1900. The turn of the century.

Night. A dying young woman leaves her child in a country church vestibule.

A heart-wrenching tale of loss, survival, and the search for belonging.

ORPHAN

The Story of Tyler Braun

MARK GENGLER

Titles by Mark Gengler

THANKS A LOT GOD

– OUR ANCESTORS SERIES –

NOAH THORNE
A WISCONSIN FARM BOY IN THE 1920'S

WOLF CREEK CIDER
THE STORY OF AARON STROUD

MIGRANT!
THE STORY OF DANNY BROOME

MARSHFIELD 1919
THE STORY OF WAYNE SCHOOLEY

ORPHAN
THE STORY OF TYLER BRAUN

*This novel is dedicated to veterans and law enforcement,
who literally put their life on the line while in uniform.*

*I have relatives who have served in both,
and I hold them in very high regard.*

*In the words of John F. Kennedy,
"Ask not what your country can do for you,
but what you can you do for your country."*

1900. The turn of the century.

Night. A dying young woman leaves her child in a country church vestibule.

A heart-wrenching tale of loss, survival, and the search for belonging.

ORPHAN

The Story of Tyler Braun

MARK GENGLER

ORPHAN *The Story of Tyler Braun*
by Mark Gengler
Our Ancestors series

Copyright © 2023 by Mark Gengler
All rights reserved.
First Edition © 2023

Published by

 SOUL FIRE PRESS
an imprint of First Steps Publishing
PO Box 571 • Gleneden Beach, OR 97388
FirstStepsPublishing.com

Interior layout, cover design by Suzanne Parrott
Cover art *Old Country Church* © 2023 Suzanne Parrott

Young Adult, 1900s, Early 20th Century historical fiction, Wisconsin, orphan, rural life, Spanish influenza, prohibition, romance, friendship

ISBN: 978-1-944072-85-8 (pb)
          978-1-944072-86-5 (epub)

10 9 8 7 6 5 4 3 2 1

Printed in the
United States of America

ACKNOWLEDGMENTS

This story came about from a comment I overheard while having a beer at my local pub. It stuck in the back of my mind until I began to build on it.

I believe I may have lived back around 1900, because I understand the time and the people. Autos were just becoming popular as the horse and buggy days were fading. People relied on each other and lived a slower, more meaningful life. My paternal grandfather was a logger, and I would listen as he told stories of life in a logging camp.

In 1920, law enforcement had no lights and sirens to stop crime. The era of prohibition was just starting, and local law officers dealt with criminals as best they could.

I hope you like reading about how your ancestors lived and worked, I certainly enjoy writing about them!

CHAPTER ONE

The young woman shuffled slowly along the gravel road, stopping often to catch her breath. A pale crescent moon cast a meager light as she moved toward her destination. It was early June, and the night air held a slight chill. She covered her ragged hacking cough with the faded blue handkerchief clutched in her left hand. In the crook of her right arm rested a baby wrapped in a thin blanket. The baby was not asleep but made no sound other than an occasional cooing whisper. Stopping and raising her head, the woman saw the steeple of the Catholic church framed against the sky. A lone tear rolled down her cheek as she neared the church steps. With great effort, she climbed one step at a time, until reaching the door. Her shaking hand tried the latch, and the door opened quietly. Stepping inside, the woman looked for the wooden box she knew was there. The box was lined with straw, and a blanket lay neatly folded at the head. The woman unfolded the blanket and gently laid the baby on it. Taking a folded note from her dress pocket, she pinned it to the blanket. Then, she leaned down and softly kissed the baby on the forehead. Rising slowly, the woman turned, shuffled out, and gently closed the door.

It was 1900, and Fitchburg, Wisconsin was slowly growing into a town. The fertile loam soil had attracted the immigrant Norwegian, German, and Irish farmers to settle and raise families. Soon a store and feed mill were built, followed by a school and two churches: one Catholic and one Lutheran. A bank and a harness shop followed. Dairy cows fed in the lush pastures alongside the large workhorses used to till the land. The milk was hauled to Madison every day, including Sunday. Life was hard, sometimes brutal, but still a better life than the one each had left behind.

Sister Ingrid always rose before sunrise. She loved the morning stillness, the peaceful beginning of each day. One of her morning chores was to check the church vestry for any milk, eggs, or canned vegetables that often were left for her, two other nuns, and Father Murphy. This morning she was surprised when she saw the baby sleeping in the wooden box. The box had been placed there five years ago after they found a baby left on the vestry floor. Sister Catherine, the senior of the three nuns, had convinced Father Murphy it was likely to happen again and that it was best to be prepared. Since then, one other baby had been found. Sister Ingrid gently picked up the baby, whispered a prayer for the mother, and took the baby to the living quarters behind the church.

In the kitchen, Sister Rose was cooking oatmeal for breakfast. She hummed as she worked, a song her mother had sung to her called 'Galway Bay.' She turned when she heard the door open and gave a slight gasp.

"Another gift from God," said Sister Ingrid with a smile. The baby waved two tiny fists in the air and began crying.

"The poor thing must be hungry," Rose said. "I'll fix a bottle of milk. We best let Sister Catherine know."

Before Ingrid could turn to leave, Catherine entered from the church. Without a word, she took the baby from Ingrid. "A bath and a change of diaper before feeding," she said. "This little one hasn't had either in a while."

Rose saw the note pinned to the blanket. "Let's see if this wee one has a name," she said as she unpinned and opened the note. The note read: Tyler Braun born May 30, 1900. Father is dead, I am very ill. Please care for him. The note was unsigned.

"We will do what we can for now, "Catherine said, "and later, Father Murphy can take him to the Foundling home in Madison."

Eugene and Joan McKinney owned a small boot & shoe repair shop on the east side of Madison. With no children of their own, Father Murphy had encouraged them to care for abandoned babies. At present, they had a boy they had named Thomas, almost a year old, who had been left at the train station. A girl named Mary had been delivered to them by a policeman six days ago. She had been found in a wicker basket at a cheap boarding house room with a pink ribbon with the name 'Mary' tied around one tiny wrist.

"We know more about this baby than any other we have ever taken in," said Joan as she read the note Father Murphy handed her. Putting the note in her apron pocket, Joan took the baby from Sister Rose. Father Murphy and Rose had left the church right after mass and arrived in Madison just after noon by horse and buggy.

"Stay and have lunch," Eugene implored.

"Maybe just a sandwich, then we must be on our way back," Father Murphy stated firmly.

Watching Joan, Sister Rose sensed the love and care this child would receive. She also knew the baby would someday be in the care of the Sisters of Mercy Orphanage. When the child was weaned and eating on its own, the Sisters of mercy took over the care of foundlings. At present, it was the only orphanage run by the Catholic Church in Madison. There was another, operated by the City of Madison, but few kind words were spoken on its behalf. After sandwiches and coffee, Father Murphy and Rose were back in the buggy and headed home.

CHAPTER TWO

By 1906 Tyler Braun had grown happy and healthy in the care of the McKinney's. Today was the 5th of May. Tyler and Mary were packing their few belongings for the move to the orphanage. His blonde hair and blue eyes told of his German heritage. Mary was an angel, her dark brown hair and gray-flecked hazel eyes suggested possible Dutch parentage. The two were best friends. At five years old they had stayed at the foundling home longer than usual. Joan McKinney had become very attached to them and was reluctant to let them go. Eugene felt the same, but knew the parting must come. They had recently taken in two babies whose parents had been killed in a garment factory fire. Joan, knowing her focus must be on the new arrivals, finally agreed to let Tyler and Mary go.

"Do you think the new sisters will like us?" Mary asked.

Thinking a moment, Tyler answered, "They have to like us because God wants them to."

Mother Superior Veronica was waiting on the front porch as Eugene arrived in his horse-drawn spring wagon. Taller than most women, Mother Veronica stood at an even six foot. Walking slowly down the porch steps, she greeted the children.

"We have been waiting for you," she said with a smile. The children climbed down from the wagon and stood before her, holding their small bundles of clothing. Eugene nodded, tipped his hat, and turned the horse around and left. He knew if he stayed any longer he might change his mind.

"Come along and I will show you your new home," said Veronica softly. Taking their small hands in each of her own, she led them up the steps and into the orphanage.

In 1907, Mary was adopted by Cecil and Regina Anderson. Their five year old daughter Ellen had died six months before from a rare kidney disease. It had been a difficult birth for Regina, and her doctor warned her that another pregnancy could result in her death. They knew about the orphanage from Father Hennesy, whose church they attended. On their first visit, Mother Veronica introduced them to Mary. Although quite shy, Mary slowly warmed to the couple who were captivated by her. It took six weeks for the court to legalize the adoption, and the orphan became Mary Anderson, with one condition. Mary insisted on being able to stay in touch with Tyler.

"He is my best friend," she said, "and I don't want to lose him." With a promise from mother Veronica and the Anderson's, Mary left for her new home.

Tyler did well in school, his quick mind soaking up knowledge like a dry sponge. Baseball and football were his favorite sports and he excelled in both. By 1912, he was growing into a sturdy youth. He took a job after school cleaning the stables at the livery barn. He had an easy way with the horses and enjoyed being around them. Their size did not seem to matter to Tyler, the horses sensed this and responded in kind.

Then he learned to saddle a horse and harness a team, the livery owner, Angus MacBain, soon had Tyler running errands with a horse and buggy. Twice a month, on Sunday afternoons, Angus allowed Tyler the use of a horse and buggy. The Anderson's lived on the west side of Madison, and Tyler would visit them and Mary. Sometimes the two young people would take a ride to Lake Mendota, sometimes a slow walk through the fields of wild flowers, and if the weather was bad, they would sit on the wide front porch and play checkers. After a Sunday supper with the family, Tyler would leave with the unspoken promise to return.

When the United States entered the World War in 1917, Tyler enlisted in the 32nd Infantry. Mother Veronica gave him her blessing, then went to her room and prayed for his safe return. Mary cried. It was the first time Tyler had ever seen her cry, and he took her in his arms, gently patting her back, telling her he would be back. They were both seventeen years old, and although the words had never been spoken, they both knew they would marry someday. The bond they shared was as soft as a rose petal and stronger than tempered steel.

Mary had grown into a lovely young woman. She was now five feet 4 inches tall, slim and graceful with a shy smile. Tyler stood an even six foot, broad at the shoulders. His blonde hair curled around his ears and his blue eyes twinkled when he laughed. When Mary had dried her eyes, she gently took Tyler's tanned face in her hands, slowly pulled his head down and they shared their first kiss.

Along with other units from Michigan, the 32nd Infantry left Wisconsin to train at Camp MacArthur, just outside of Waco, Texas. Armed with the Springfield 1903 bolt action rifle, they trained in military tactics last used in the Civil War. Some of these tactics would never be used in the new modern warfare, other tactics were timeless and would save lives. Marching, field drills, hand-to-hand combat, bayonet drills and much time on the firing range. Surviving the Texas heat soon toughened the men, binding them together as a combat ready unit.

In February of 1918, the 32nd infantry arrived in France. The French and British commanders wanted to split the unit up to bolster their own depleted ranks, but General John 'Black Jack' Pershing would not agree.

"These men fight together as one, and will prove their worth in battle," he said firmly and his words soon came true. In their first conflict, the 32nd drove through the Hindenburg line, the first allied force to fight the enemy on his own ground, and win. Their unit patch became the red arrow crossing a red line. They took casualties, but never retreated or gave back ground captured.

No wagon or motorized vehicle could travel the rough shell-holed terrain. Teams of pack mules supplied them with food, clothing and ammunition, while the local water was boiled for drinking and cooking. Smokers now used a pipe with a tin cap on the bowl so no pin-prick light of a cigarette or cigar could be detected. Bayonets were kept sharp enough to shave with and rifles were cleaned whenever possible.

Private First Class Tyler Braun became the best shot in his unit. Taking out a German machine gun crew at two hundred yards, his platoon was able to gain a position upward of a German trench. Knowing surrender was their only option, two hundred German soldiers and officers lay down their guns, raised their hands, and were marched to the rear to become prisoners of war. A week later, a newly promoted Corporal Braun sewed on his new stripes.

Three young goats had been purchased from a local farmer and the soldiers thrived on the much needed fresh meat. The cook was an Irishman from Michigan who had worked in the kitchen of a fine hotel. He saved every scrap of meat and brewed up a tasty stew with the leftovers. The medical officer was kept busy, checking the soldiers every day for a variety of ailments. He pulled teeth, lanced boils, bandaged cuts and removed splinters. All too soon, this would change.

CHAPTER THREE

Tyler woke early on the morning of July 15th, 1918. It was still dark. The 32nd was dug in on the French flank of the Marne River. Things had been fairly quiet during the last two weeks, which made the officers uneasy. They had kept the unit alert, changing guards often to keep the men on their toes. A morning mist hung over the river. It would be another hot day Tyler thought as he pulled on his boots. Suddenly the guards shouted. "Boats on the river!" Then the shooting began!

Hundreds of German assault troops appeared out of the mist. The French, British, and American troops formed their battle lines and the war was on! The first line of the allied defense was over run in some places, but the second line was higher up behind a railroad embankment, and was able to hold their position. The American Commander called for reinforcements, and by the second day the assault had ground to a halt.

The battle lasted for another day, and when allied forces arrived, the Germans began to withdraw, having suffered heavy casualties. Tyler and several others who had not been injured, helped to load the wounded in wagons to be taken to the field hospital in the rear.

Later he sat down to write Mary a letter, but his hands were shaking so badly he balled up the paper and threw it away. Like so many other young men, the memory of this battle would stay with him forever.

More ships from America were arriving at the ports of France bringing reinforcements that filled out the ranks of the 32nd along with much needed supplies and ammunition. The artillery units stocked up on the large shells. Medical supplies were loaded in ambulances and transported to the front. Cases of canned vegetables and meat were taken to the kitchens. Bales of new uniforms were made available, along with boots and helmets. Infantry units like the 32nd that were almost constantly on the move would eventually get what they needed.

Tyler wrote to Mary as often as he could. He described the countryside they traveled through, the people they met, the food and the weather. He told her about the men in his platoon and where they were from. He did not tell her about the bloody battles or the constant shelling done by both sides.

Mother Veronica got a letter about once a month. Tyler would tell her about the churches they saw and describe the statues and stained glass windows. He did not mention the rapidly filling graveyards or the starving families driven from their homes by the war.

Waiting at home, Mary followed the war by reading the newspapers. Tyler's letters let her know he was still alive, but she wanted to know about the battles and the progress of the 32nd Infantry. The battle at the Marne River was reported in great detail, telling Mary what really happened. She prayed each night for Tyler's safe return, and saved every letter.

Miles away at the Orphanage, Mother Veronica did the same. Several young men she had sent out into the world were fighting in the war. Some Army, some Navy and three were piloting airplanes. At Vespers each evening a special prayer was said for them.

The German army was in retreat. The tanks had turned the tide of war in favor of the allies. All through August, the French and British soldiers had crawled from the trenches to fight the enemy on his own ground. The German army was running out of food, ammunition and men. By September 1918, they had been pushed back to the Meuse River. With the Argonne Forest as their only protection, they dug in. General Pershing met with the commanders of the French and British forces and stated, "a full scale assault is our only option." Reserve troops were brought up to fill out the ranks, and on September 27th, the largest and longest battle of the war began. With the 32nd Infantry leading the way, thousands of allied troops stormed the Argonne Forest.

The battle raged for 47 days. Knowing defeat was inevitable, Germany finally gave up. On the 11th hour of the 11th day of the 11th month, 1918, the armistice was signed and the Great War was over. Over a million soldiers had died, along with thousands of civilians. Farm fields that once had grown food to feed a nation were now shell-holed, war torn soil that would take years to reclaim. Trenches would have to be filled and for years skeletons would turn up, along with broken rifles and rusty helmets, as fields were plowed.

Sergeant Tyler Braun was among those decorated for bravely in battle. At a great ceremony in Paris, medals were pinned on proud men—French, British and American. Tyler had led his platoon in an attack on a German stronghold, and captured fifty five-crack German troops. As men gathered later to celebrate, they held a long moment of silent prayer for the fallen.

Troop ships began leaving the ports of France in late December. Field hospitals were emptied as the wounded were loaded aboard and headed out to sea, bound for America. Tons of American war supplies that had been waiting to be unloaded, turned around and left for home. By January 1919, Tyler Braun and thousands of soldiers finally were able to leave France on the USS Hampton. None knew they were bringing death with them.

CHAPTER FOUR

It began with a tickle in the throat. A runny nose and a slight fever, just like a common cold. Within 24 hours the lungs filled with thick fluid and the fever could reach 104 degrees. Eight out of ten people died within 48 to 72 hours. Doctors were frantic to find a cure. They poured over medical journals looking for anything that could help. It was called influenza, but a strain never experienced before. It took lives at random. Young, old, rich, poor, sick, healthy, and no race of people were immune. Doctors and nurses died along with their patients. Entire families could be wiped out in a week. As the death toll rose, shiploads of returning soldiers entered the ports of New York and New Jersey, bringing more death.

Tyler and his friend Louis Porter were on deck when the Statue of Liberty was sighted. A great yell went up from all around them.

"Lady Liberty is here to welcome us home," Louis said laughing.

"I can't wait to get off of this ship," said Tyler. "I want to get started home to Madison."

"I'm traveling on to Eau Claire, but let's keep in touch." The two soldiers met just before the Meuse-Argonne battle. Louis had been one of the replacements brought in to fill out the ranks. As soldiers always do, he had asked around if there were any other men from his home town. "Sergeant Braun is from Madison," someone told him. The two men had become good friends.

The Porter family raised and sold horses. "My granddad started with Percherons," Louis said, "but dad added the Belgians because farmers kept asking for them."

"I sure would like to see your horses," Tyler told him. "Maybe after I take care of some things at home, I'll come visit."

From the Port Authority, the soldiers boarded the train for Fort Meade, Maryland to turn in their gear and receive their final pay. Tyler noticed that Louis was coughing and sweating.

"Better see the Doctor right away," Tyler said.

"It's just a cold," Louis insisted. "I'll be fine in a few days." Doctors were waiting to examine every arriving soldier. Seven out of ten men were culled from the ranks and sent to the hospital. It was the last time Tyler would see his friend Louis. After getting his pay and signing his separation papers, Tyler bought a ticket for Madison, Wisconsin. He was on his way home to see Mary.

It was snowing when the Great Northern Limited left the station. The newspaper Tyler bought told of the deadly flu sweeping across the country. A small town in Iowa with a population of 400 was almost entirely wiped out. Only six people survived. There were no funerals held. The graves were marked with a wooden cross bearing the name age, and date of death, with the location marked in the register.

Funerals would be held later after the deadly virus had passed. Headstones would replace the crosses, and those who survived would mourn the dead.

Changing trains in Chicago, Tyler headed northwest to Madison. He had not had a letter from Mary since November. He prayed he would find her safe and well, but an anxious feeling gnawed at his heart. In the early morning light the silent farm fields lay under a blanket of snow. The train made several stops at small town stations, dropping off and picking up passengers and luggage. A middle-aged couple dressed entirely in black boarded. A black veil covered the woman's face, the husband held her as she silently wept. They both seemed almost too tired to walk, shuffling their feet as they moved. No one talked. Each person was lost in their own world of grief at a loved ones passing.

Arriving in Madison, Tyler's first stop was the orphanage. He needed to be assured that Mother Superior Veronica was still alive and well. She was the only parentage figure in his life, the one who had nourished and guided him to adulthood. Their bond was strong, broken only by death. A young novice greeted him and took him to the chapel where Mother Veronica waited. The chapel was hushed, the lingering scent of incense hung in the air. Tyler silently waited as Mother Veronica finished her prayers, rose and greeted him.

"Such a handsome young man you have become," she said with a smile.

"I am so glad you are alive and well," Tyler said, "is there any word from Mary?"

Taking his hands in hers, Veronica said softly "Mary and

her parents died from the flu almost a month ago. I wrote you, but the letter must not have reached you. They are buried in the cemetery at Saint Paul's church."

Tyler slowly sank into a pew as tears filled his eyes. Mother Veronica held him as he wept for the young woman he had loved. Taking a handkerchief from her sleeve, she pressed it into Tyler's palm.

Raising his tear-stained face, he whispered, "How will I go on without her?"

"You will do as you have always done," she said. "You will place your life and future in God's hands. You will pray each day for the strength to move forward, and pray each night that tomorrow will be better."

Tyler got a room at the Bradford Hotel, a modest three-story dwelling with a bathroom at the end of each hallway and the Crown Café located two doors down from the hotel. Tyler lay down on the single bed, closed his eyes and slept. He awoke in the gray dawn, still in his uniform, boots on his feet. He rose slowly, undressed, and looked in the mirror above the dresser, shocked by the haggard face with red-rimmed eyes staring back at him. Wrapping a towel around himself, he picked up his shaving kit and walked down the hall to the bathroom.

A hot bath and a shave bought him back among the living. Back in his room, Tyler took stock of his situation. He would have to wear his uniform until the stores opened and he could buy some warm civilian clothing. Dressing, he headed to the Cafe.

After a breakfast of coffee, pancakes and sausage, Tyler went in search of a clothing store. He bought wool shirts, trousers, stockings, mittens and a cap. The uniform he would have cleaned and stow it in his duffel bag. His Army overcoat would serve as a warm winter coat. A plan was forming in his mind. He would leave Madison for Eau Claire and find his friend Louis Porter. Tyler thought that working with horses would help heal the empty spot in his heart left by Mary's death.

Pulling a chair up next to the dresser, Tyler wrote a letter to Mother Superior Veronica, telling her of his journey to Eau Claire. He explained that he could not stay in Madison, but that he would try to find a way to heal his broken spirit. He told her about his friend Louis Porter and the horses. In closing he said he would keep in touch and thanked her for all she had done for him.

Tyler mailed the letter on his way to the railroad station. It was three in the afternoon on a cold windy day. The train would leave at five, giving Tyler time for a meal. As he ate, he read the paper he had bought. The deadly flu virus was now world-wide, threatening the national economy and the rebuilding of France and Germany.

CHAPTER FIVE

The sun was just a yellow ball in the sky, giving off no warmth. Jackson Porter leaned on the corral fence, left foot on the bottom rail, arms crossed on the top rail. At 52 years old, he was still lean. All 5 foot 10 inches of him was wiry muscle. His brown hair was showing some gray, but his brown eyes were sharp and clear. He was watching the three Percheron mares, out for some exercise. Two of the mares would foal in late spring, along with one of the Belgian mares. Jack, as he was known by everyone on the farm, kept twelve horses over the winter, six mares and six stallions. Automobiles and tractors were becoming popular with farmers, but there were still places a truck or tractor could not go.

People will always need horses, thought Jack. Then, he motioned to his foreman Tom Willet, "Put them back in the stable Tom," he called, "then come in for supper."

As Jack turned from the corral, he noticed a figure walking up the long driveway. A man on foot in the dead of winter was not a usual sight. This one walked with his head down, moving slowly toward the farmhouse.

Jack met him as he reached the porch, holding out his hand. "Welcome stranger, what brings you out this way?"

Raising his head the man shook the offered hand. "Hello Mr. Porter, my name is Tyler Braun. I served in the 32nd infantry with Louis. He said I should visit him someday. Is he here?"

Jack's face went pale as he stared at the young man in front of him. In a hushed voice he said, "Come in the house and get warm. Have supper with us, and then we must have a long talk."

The big open kitchen was warm, with the delicious aroma of chicken and dumplings. A platter of hot cornbread squares and a bowl of green beans sat waiting on the red checkered tablecloth. Around the table sat Tom Willet, his wife Julia, who did the cooking, and the blacksmith, Andy Schwanke, his bald head shining from the overhead light.

"We have a guest," said Tom, as Tyler removed his overcoat and cap.

"Set another plate Julia," Jack said. "This is Tyler Braun. Tyler served in France with Louis."

Tom and Andy rose, and shook Tyler's hand. Julia set another plate, silverware and coffee mug while Jack bought in another chair.

Tyler sat, looked around, and asked "Isn't Louis here?"

"I will tell you all about Louis after we eat" Jack said, "you must be hungry after the long walk from the train station."

The meal finished, Julia poured coffee for everyone. Jack packed and lit his pipe.

"When was the last time you saw Louis, Tyler?" Jack asked.

"At Fort Meade. He had a cough and cold, so the doctors took him to the hospital."

Jack nodded his head slowly. "Louis died at the Fort Meade hospital from the flu. I'm surprised and glad that you didn't catch it."

Tyler's eyes misted over and he slowly shook his head. "I lost the girl I was going to marry to the flu," Tyler said softly.

With his hand on Tyler's shoulder, Jack said, "My wife Clara and our daughter Carol died two months ago from the flu."

Tom Willet spoke up. "Julia and I lost our daughter, Theresa, at the same time." For a time, there was a silence, broken only by the ticking of the wall clock, then Jack spoke. "You will stay the night," he said, "and tomorrow we will show you what we do here."

Julia was up before sunrise, as usual. Her blonde hair was threaded with gray now, and she had gained a few pounds that did not want to go away. Since the death of Jack's wife and daughter, Julia and Tom had moved into the Porter house at Jack's insistence. They worried for him as he worried for them. This morning, breakfast would be more than usual. The young man who had arrived last night had the haunted look of a lost soul. He was also in need of the meals he had missed. Fried potatoes, bacon, eggs, biscuits and coffee should begin to add the pounds he needed. As Julia worked, she caught herself humming an old tune, something she had not done in months. Smiling, she thought, 'maybe this young man can put some new life back into an old family.'

Andy Schwanke came in, stomped the snow off his boots in the mudroom, and sat at the table. Standing 5 foot seven, he was almost as wide as he was tall, without an ounce of fat.

He had his own room off the tack room of the blacksmith shop. The pot-bellied stove kept him warm at night, and he was there if the horses needed anything.

"Got about an inch of new snow last night. And Molly is taking care of the mares, just like a nursemaid," he said with a smile as Julia poured him a cup of coffee. Molly was Andy's border collie. She had never had a litter of her own, so she mothered the mares, who accepted her without question.

Tom entered the kitchen, took a deep breath and smiled. "I can't remember the last time we had fresh biscuits," he said. "Must be a special day."

"Nothing special," said Julia. "I just felt like making them."

"And when breakfast is over there won't be a biscuit left," Jack said as he entered and sat down.

Slowly, almost shyly, Tyler entered. "Good morning," he said. "Sure smells good in here.

"That's because I married the finest cook this side of the Mississippi," Tom said. Jack poured coffee all around as Julia set the food on the table. Everyone clasped their hands as Andy said grace.

Molly came running from the stables as the men left the house. Seeing Tyler she stopped and approached slowly. "Just hold still and let her sniff you," Tom said. "If she likes you, she'll let you know."

Molly sniffed Tyler's legs, sat, and held out her paw. Gently, Tyler shook it. "Hello, Molly. I'm Tyler." With a soft 'woof', Molly greeted the others.

"I'm going to let the big boys out while I clean the stalls," Tom said. Standing at the rail with Jack, Tyler watched as three huge Percherons walked out into the fresh snow. One was dark brown, one a lighter brown and the last a dark gray. Tyler was entranced, a smile slowly formed on his face as the horses kicked at the fresh snow. Easing himself through the corral fence, Tyler approached the giants. They snuffled at him as he began scratching their foreheads.

"You have worked with horses before," Jack said.

"I worked at a stable in Madison before I joined the Army," said Tyler. "I like being around horses."

"And they seem to like you." Jack grinned as the Belgians came out next, all three dark brown with blonde manes. "Tyler, Let's go check on the mares."

Tyler followed him into the stable. The mare in foal was easy to spot. All three poked their heads over the stable doors hoping for a treat. Jack dipped his hand into his pocket and gave each a cube of sugar.

Then, as he gave the Percheron mares their treat, he turned toward Tyler. "Let's see what Andy is working on this morning."

In the blacksmith shop, Andy was heating up the forge. "We need some new hinges on the stable doors and then I have to mend a bent wagon hitch."

"Can I help?" asked Tyler. "I was going to learn the trade before the war broke out."

"I would be glad for the help," Andy said with a grin.

Jack nodded. "Then I'll leave you two to work, and I'll give Tom a hand with the horses."

Lunch was a chicken stew made from the leftover chicken and dumplings.

"What's for supper, Julia?" Tom asked.

"We're having ham with butternut squash and fresh bread tonight," she said.

Pointing at the corner of Tyler's mouth, Jack laughed. "I see a little spot of drool there, Tyler."

Smiling, Tyler murmured, "And I think my stomach is grumbling too."

Everyone laughed, the first laughter heard in the house in months. Looking around, Tyler did not feel like a stranger. He felt as part of the group, a feeling not felt since leaving the 32nd Infantry. He had no reason to return to Madison, he could do as his head and heart wished. At this moment, he wished he could stay.

After supper that night, Jack pushed back his chair and lit his pipe.

"Tom, Julia, Andy and I talked about you today," he said to Tyler. "We all agree that we want you to stay on here as long as you wish. What do you say?"

Tyler looked around at each one, then spoke. "I'm an orphan, raised by Catholic nuns after I was left in a church. I have no real family now that my Mary is gone. I am glad you wish me to stay, because I wish to stay also." A tear slowly eased its way down Julia's cheek as Tom cleared his throat.

"Louis's room will be yours," Jack said, "Welcome to our family."

The days passed quickly as Tyler made himself useful. He learned to prepare the forge, work the bellows, shape horseshoes and fuse broken metal. Every tool in the shop had a purpose and Andy taught Tyler their names and uses.

When Molly wasn't busy with the mares, she followed Tyler like a little sister, craving his attention. Tyler had a calming effect on the horses. He was never in a hurry with them, always patient and gentle. At times, he would find a new article of clothing replacing something of his that had worn out. Socks, a pair of long underwear, a wool shirt. He asked Julia, who said, "just some things of Louis's that Jack thought you could use."

A feeling of belonging was forming in Tyler, and he welcomed it.

CHAPTER SIX

The blizzard blew into Eau Claire on March 5th. The wind piled drifts against anything that did not move. The sun rose and set behind the whirling snow without ever revealing itself. Schools had closed the day before, and teachers told students not to expect classes to resume until roads were cleared. Businesses across the state would not open again until March 10th. At the Porter farm, the horses were given extra hay and grain. Extra water buckets were set out and the stalls were cleaned.

"March storms are always the worst," Jack said, "like an angry man getting in the last word of an argument."

Additional firewood was bought in and piled in the mudroom for Julia. The aroma of fresh baked bread and beef stew dominated the kitchen. Andy and Molly would spend the night in their room at the shop. Tom had taken a covered pot of stew and a loaf of bread out to them. Around the table that evening everyone told stories of storms they remembered. Tyler told of his last winter in France, and the heavy snowfall just a week after the Meuse-Argonne battle ended. Everyone slept well that night as the coal-fired furnace in the basement kept them warm.

It took days to dig out from the blizzard, the drifts against the stable doors were cleared first, then a team of Belgians was harnessed to a homemade plow to clear the driveway out to the county road. Snow plow drivers earned their money that week, busting through drifts and working twelve and sometimes fourteen hours at a time. Milk trucks often passed by a farm, unable to get in and pick up the milk. Mail delivery did not resume for a week, and doctors fretted over patients they could not get to. Eventually, life returned to normal, as the winter of 1919 shook off its wintery weather and began the long trek to spring.

Lying prone behind the Percheron mare, Jack grabbed the forefeet as the foal began to emerge. "Push girl, push!" With a half groan, half grunt, the mare gave a final mighty push. The foal slid down onto the bed of straw. Molly was up front licking the mare around the face.

"Get her on her feet Tom," Jack said, "this baby is already standing." On wobbly legs, the foal stood as Jack and Tyler wiped it's face and flanks. In no time at all, the foal had found the milk source and was feeding. The other Percheron mare had foaled the week before, with no problems. It was the first week of April. The weather was still cold at night, but warming during the day.

Jack and Tom rolled the shed doors open wide. "Time to get the truck on the road," Jack said. Tyler watched as the two men secured the battery, checked the oil and poured gas in the tank. It was a 1917 Dodge half-ton flatbed that had been well taken care of. Jack got behind the wheel as Tom got ready to turn the crank. Working the choke, Jack hollered "ready!" Tom leaned hard into the crank, and on the second turn the motor started. It ran a little rough at first, but soon smoothed out.

Jack drove to the front of the house and parked, letting the motor idle. As he got out, Julia stood on the porch waiting.

"We're low on almost everything in the pantry," she said, "Tom and I are going into Eau Claire to stock up. Is there anything you need, Tyler?"

"Some shaving soap and maybe a newspaper," Tyler said.

"I'll bring back three newspapers," Julia said. "Jack will be looking for horse sales and auctions."

After supper that evening, Jack spread a newspaper out on the kitchen table. "A man in Cedar Falls has a four year old Belgian mare for sale," he said, "might be worth looking at."

With a wry smile Julia pointed out, "if you would finally get a telephone installed, you could call him."

With a sheepish grin Jack replied, "I guess it would save us some wasted trips. I'll go into Eau Claire tomorrow and see to it."

"No need," Julia said. "I talked to the man at the telephone company today. He'll be here tomorrow."

Tyler, grinning like a milk-fed cat said, "Ain't progress wonderful, Jack?"

The telephone changed the way the Porter family did business. By the first of May, Jack and Tom had found and purchased a five year old male Percheron and two four-year-old Belgians, both mares. The weather was warm, mid-sixties during the day, and around forty at night. The pastures were a lush green carpet, and the fields of alfalfa would soon be ready for the first cut of hay. The mower and the hay loader

36

were greased and ready to go. The hay mows were almost empty. What was left got cleared out to make way for the new crop. The garden plot was plowed up and harrowed, soon to be planted.

The Dodge truck drove slowly into the drive, towing the horse trailer. It came to a stop by the corral and Tom and Tyler got out slowly. It had been a long trip to La Cross, but Tom had gotten a good deal on a team of six-year-old Percherons, a male and a female. Jack waited by the gate as the horses were unloaded.

"They both need hooves trimmed and new shoes," Tom said, "otherwise they are in fine shape."

"Sold a team of Belgians while you were gone." Jack said. "Circus World at Baraboo is getting ready to go on the road. They will take this team also."

Looking a bit confused, Tyler asked, "Doesn't the Circus travel by rail?"

Tom spoke up. "The wagons need the teams to get them to the railroad yard. They help load the heavy wagons onto flatbed rail-cars, then unload them at their destination. The horses also help put up the big tents and bring in loads of hay and straw."

Nodding his head, Tyler said, "I guess there is a lot to learn about the Circus."

"When this team is ready," Jack said, "you and I will take it to Baraboo. It will give you an idea how much people still need horses."

Supper that night was corned beef and cabbage with rye bread. Later, having coffee, Jack asked "What's the date today, Julia?"

"It's May 30th," she said with a smile. Rising from her chair, Julia went to the pantry and returned with a chocolate cake lit with 19 candles. Setting it on the table she said, "Happy Birthday, Tyler."

Jack, Tom and Andy chimed in singing happy birthday.

"How did you know it was my birthday?" asked Tyler, blushing and grinning at the same time.

"You told us about the orphanage when you first got here," Julia said, "so I called and spoke to Mother Superior Veronica. She told me about the note pinned to your blanket. She also wishes you to write her more often."

Reaching in his pocket, Andy handed Tyler a tissue-wrapped gift. Tyler opened it to find a belt buckle in the shape of a horseshoe. "That is from me and Molly," he said.

Tom handed Tyler a small box, saying, "Julia and I want you to have this."

Opening the box, Tyler drew out a pocket watch on a light chain. "It's the first watch I ever owned, thank you," Tyler said.

From his shirt pocket, Jack took out a small leather pouch and handed it to Tyler. Pulling open the drawstring, Tyler tipped the pouch open and a key fell out into his hand. "The key is to this house," Jack said. "It means you will always have a home here."

Tyler's eyes misted over and he was at a loss for words. Julia saved the moment saying "Jack, you slice up the cake, and make sure Tyler gets the biggest piece!"

CHAPTER SEVEN

It was an experience Tyler would never forget. He had gone with Jack to deliver the team of Percheron's to the circus at Baraboo. Driving onto the circus's winter home site, Jack explained "Seven Ringling brothers started this whole thing with one wagon, one tent and a rented team of horses. That was back in 1884, and look at it now." The wagons alone were enough to boggle the mind. Brightly painted in every color known to man, they were rolling works of art. Animals Tyler had never seen before walked past him. zebras, camels, elephants, ostrich's, and some Tyler did not know the names of. In cages were tigers, lions, bears, monkeys, gorillas, and beautiful rare birds.

A large man approached holding a clipboard. Smiling, he shook Jack's hand. "You got here just in time. We are loading for our opening show in Chicago."

Tyler helped unload the horses from the trailer. Looking them over, the man nodded his head. "Fine looking team," he said as he handed Jack an envelope. "Stay and have lunch with us," he said pointing to one of the open tents.

"Thanks, we will" Jack said.

On an open grill, two women were roasting chickens. A buffet table was groaning under the weight of baked potatoes, salads, bread, and several pies cut into slices. Getting cups of coffee, Jack and Tyler loaded up a plate and sat. A man covered in tattoos sat next to Tyler. Next to Jack was a lady with a beard. Across the table was the biggest man they had ever seen. He was bald and his huge arms rippled with muscle. Next to him was a man who must have been eight feet tall. All were talking about the upcoming show in Chicago. It was a day Tyler would never forget.

Over supper that night, Tyler Told Julia, Tom and Andy about all he had seen. There were several comments of "I can hardly believe it!" and "can you imagine that!"

"I also heard that the Ringling Brothers are buying the Barnum & Bailey Circus," Jack said, "it will make them the largest circus in North America."

"Will they need more horses?" Tom asked.

"I already have a standing order for two more teams," said Jack.

The first crop of hay was ready. Jack was mowing with the Farmall tractor and Tom driving a team of Belgians towing a wagon with a hay-loader behind. Jack had hired two boys from town to help with the hay. Tyler was busy helping Julia with the garden. Another team of Belgians was in the corral. Andy was getting ready to shoe them after trimming the hooves. Molly was watching over the new colts as they kicked up their heels in the pasture. Summer was in full swing at the Porter farm.

Tom and Tyler were washing up at the water tank by the corral when two big trucks pulled into the yard. The second truck was blowing a big cloud of steam from the front. A lean man wearing a suit got out of the first truck and approached Tom.

"We got some engine trouble," he said. "Can you help us?"

"Let me take a look," Tom said. A puddle was forming under the front of the truck as Tom opened the hood. Tom looked down from the top, then got underneath. Crawling out he said, "you got a hole in the radiator hose. It's not something you can patch, but I can take you into Eau Claire to get a new hose."

"Will it take long?" the lean man asked.

"We can have you back on the road in about an hour," Tom told him.

"Let's do it," the man said with a smile.

"While we are gone, have your men take the old hose off. It will save us some time." While Tom went to get the Dodge, the lean man talked to the driver of the truck, who nodded his head. The driver got out, took some tools from the box on the side of the truck and crawled underneath. He reappeared shortly with the steaming hose.

Within twenty minutes Tom and the lean man returned with a new hose. The driver fitted it on and Tyler started bringing water from the pump that fed the tank. The driver started the engine and it ran fine. The lean man shook Tom's hand saying, "Thanks a lot friend."

As the trucks drove back to the highway, Tom held out his hand. "When we shook hands, he passed this to me," Tom said.

Looking down, Tyler saw a twenty dollar gold piece. Looking up at Tom, Tyler asked "Who do you suppose they were?"

"My guess would be those trucks were loaded with whiskey from Canada," Tom said, "Probably came down through Minnesota and are headed for Chicago."

At supper that night, Tom passed around the gold piece and told how he got it. "Now that you're rich, are you going to retire?" asked Andy, laughing.

Julia snatched up the coin and tucked it in her apron pocket. "This coin is going to by me something I have been wanting for years," she said.

"Is this about the mule again?" Jack asked.

"Yes, it's about the mule," Julia snapped back.

"What about a mule?" Tyler asked. "

"We always use one of the horses to cultivate the garden," Julia explained, "and their big feet trample more plants than we can spare. A mule has smaller, tougher feet and would be perfect for cultivating."

Smiling, Jack asked, "Do you just happen to know where you can get a mule?"

Blushing and grinning, Julia said, "Amos Richter has a six year old jenny he will sell for fifteen dollars."

Tom stood up and hugged his wife, saying, "Tomorrow, you and Tyler go see Amos and bring home that jenny."

"Her name is Lucy" Amos told Julia, "I have four mules now and no man needs four mules. She is a sweet gentle thing, but watch her in the garden."

"Why is that?" Julia asked.

In a loud whisper, Amos said, "She likes to eat carrot tops. She can nip them off without breaking stride."

"I will remember that," Julia said with a smile. A female mule, or jenny, is usually smaller than a male mule, called a jack. Lucy was a medium gray color with big brown eyes and dainty ears pointing straight up.

"For five dollars more, I can add the harness," Amos said.

Julia handed him the gold coin, saying, "Thank you Amos, she is just what I have been looking for."

"We are getting low on firewood," Tom mentioned over breakfast.

"You and Tyler take one of the Percheron's and the go-devil and bring down a few of the logs we cut last year," Jack said.

"What is a go-devil?" Tyler asked.

"Come with me and I will show you," said Tom.

Rolling open the shed door, Tom emerged with a low two-wheel cart with a platform on it. "We chain the butt of the logs to the platform and roll them down to the house," Tom said. "Logging operations use them all the time."

They harnessed one of the horses, grabbed an axe and set off for the woodlot. "We will take a pine and a maple," Tom said. "That should keep Julia in stove wood for quite a while."

Tyler chopped the limbs off the logs, then he and Tom lifted them onto the go-devil and chained them down. In no time they had the logs back to the house.

Andy was waiting with the two-man saw and two notched saw horses. "Me and you will saw while Tom splits the chunks" he said. The logs were about a foot across at the butt and almost twenty foot long. Lifting a log onto the saw horses, Andy and Tyler began sawing. "Just push and pull" Andy said, "once we get cutting, it will go fast."

By lunch time both logs were cut up and Tom had just a few yet to split. Jack came from the stable and nodded his head. "Good morning's work men," he said. "Let's stack it by the kitchen and get some lunch."

CHAPTER EIGHT

Galen Nichols slowly paced the platform at the railroad station in Mellen. At thirty-years-old he was stocky without being overweight. Brown hair topped a 5 foot 10 inch frame. He was waiting for the train bringing his friend and partner Elmer Krause. It was mid-July, and the thermometer on the station wall read 85 degrees. Galen had been in the Marine Corps during the war, and had met Elmer at basic training. They were both from Wausau, Wisconsin. After the war, they had decided to pool their meager resources and go into business.

"Damn trains are never on time," muttered Galen. Then, in the distance, he heard the steam whistle. Minutes later the old train eased into the station and one passenger stepped down.

"Been waiting long?" Elmer asked with a grin. The porter set down one bag, tipped his hat, climbed aboard, and the train departed. Elmer was two years younger than Galen, about the same height, but lean, with black hair.

"Let's get your bag in the truck and go, we got some miles to cover," Galen said. The Chevrolet pick-up truck started right up and the men headed north.

Their destination was an old logging camp twelve miles northeast of Mellen. Galen had leased a tract of hardwood timber, left behind when the white pine loggers went through fifteen years before. The white pine could be cut, stacked alongside the river, and floated to the mills in the spring. Not so the hardwoods. But the times were changing. Now the railroads were building spur lines into the wilderness, making it possible for loggers to cut the oaks, ash, maples and hickory, and haul them out to waiting trucks. The trucks drove them to the spur line where they were loaded onto flatbed cars and delivered to the mill. Galen and Elmer needed a base to work from, and the old camp would be it.

The dirt track leading to the camp was potholed and overgrown with weeds. An old flatbed truck was already there. Waiting for them was a big man. He stood well over six foot with heavily muscled arms. His hair was a light brown with a bushy beard to match.

Getting out of the pick-up, Galen shook the man's hand and said to Elmer, "This is Michael 'Mick' Hanlon. He will be our logging boss. How do the buildings look Mick?"

"It surprised me that most of the structures are in pretty good shape," Mick said. "The stables for the horses need some work and the roof on the equipment shed needs patching. We will need stoves for the kitchen, bunkhouse and office. Everything else just needs a good cleaning."

Scratching his head, Elmer asked, "How many horses do we need and where do we get them?"

"We want good stock that isn't going to give out on us in mid-winter," Galen told him, "and for that we go see Jackson Porter in Eau Claire."

Jack Porter's farm was known across the state for reliable draft horses. Jack and Tom were seasoned veterans at spotting a problem others had missed. At auctions and sales, they often passed up what seemed to be a great deal, opting to spend a little more for a sure thing. Although Jack bred and raised Percherons and Belgians, he bought and sold many breeds of horses, singles and teams. Some breeds worked well with others, some did not. Working with them every day helped to sort out the teams. Any man was proud to tell someone "Bought these horses from Jack Porter."

Jack and Tyler were working with a team of Suffolks Jack had bought at an estate sale two days before. Both were six-year-old geldings.

"Try backing them up, Tyler," Jack said.

"Back, boys," Tyler urged. He gave a slight tug on the reins, and the team responded, slowly backing up. "Whoa," Tyler called out. The team stopped, both gave a snort and shook their big heads.

"Someone trained these animals well," Jack said with a smile. "They will bring a good price." They heard a truck and saw the cloud of dust coming up the driveway. "This must be the guy from Mellen who called about some horses, Tyler. Let's go say hello."

"Fine looking team," Galen said as he shook Jack's hand, "Suffolks, if I'm not mistaken."

"Both six-year-old geldings," Jack said. Pointing at Tyler he said, "This is Tyler Braun, a friend of my late son, Louis. Tyler is one of the best young men with horses I have seen."

Shaking Tyler's hand, Galen said, "I've opened up an old logging camp near Mellen. I have a contract with the mill in

Wausau for all the hardwood I can send them. I've got a full crew for cutting, now I need horses to haul the logs to the trucks."

"Are you looking for teams or singles" Jack asked.

"I will need both" Galen said. "I figure two teams that can work separate if need be."

Pointing at the Suffolks, Jack said, "This team will fit the bill. I also have another team you might find interesting. Turning to Tyler, Jack smiled, saying, "Turn these boys loose and harness the team we worked with yesterday."

Grinning, Tyler said, "I'll bet he has never seen a team like this before."

While Tyler was getting the horses ready, Galen said, "I am also looking for a stable manager, someone who can properly care for the horses on a daily basis. Do you think Tyler might be interested in the job?"

Rubbing his chin a minute, Jack said, "I sure would hate to see him go, but you can ask him."

Tyler came from the stable with the most unusual team Galen had ever seen. In harness was a white Irish draft horse and a Pinto draft horse, both about the same size and weight. Scratching his head and smiling, Galen said, "I wouldn't believe it without seeing it."

"The Irish is a seven-year-old mare," Jack said. "The Pinto is a six-year-old gelding. They will work together or separate, but won't team with any other horses. I will give you a great deal on them."

"You give me a deal on them and the Suffolks and I will be a happy man," Galen said with a big grin. Turning to Tyler, Galen asked "Would you be interested in job as my stable manager for about eight months? The job pays $50 a month, $75 if you can run a forge."

Tyler was temporary speechless! His mind whirled at the thought of being out on his own, doing what he loved to do. The light in his eyes grew bright at the prospect of trying himself in a new job.

Looking at Jack, Tyler asked, "Can you spare me this winter?"

Jack saw a young man wanting to spread his wings and test himself. With a sigh he said, "I think Mr. Nichols just hired himself a teamster/blacksmith."

Galen and Tyler shook hands, and both were smiling. "Let's go up to the house," Tyler said, "we can work out the details over coffee."

At supper that night, Tyler gave everyone the news.

"When would you have to leave," Julia asked.

"Mr. Nichols wants me and the horses in Mellen on August 15th," Tyler said. "He will have the stables and the forge ready by then."

"Are they cutting right now?" asked Tom.

"They are clearing trails and getting the kitchen and bunkhouse ready," Jack said. "Galen figures they will begin cutting timber around the first of September."

"He is going to need go-devils," Andy offered. "Does he have any?"

"The mill in Wausau is sending him four," Tyler said, "two on wheels and two on ski's."

Julia was very quiet, her eyes sad, like a mother about to lose a child.

Tyler was preparing to leave the only real home he had ever known. He decided his Army uniform would stay here. Julia had it cleaned and pressed and it hung in his closet.

Into his bag went warm wool clothing he would need. Long underwear, socks, shirts pants. Julia walked in as he was packing. She handed him a thick woolen scarf, some cotton gloves and a pair of mittens.

"These should come in handy on those cold days," she said with a sad smile.

"They sure will, thank you," Tyler said.

As she left, Tom entered carrying a pair of leather boots. "My boots are a size larger than yours," he said. "With thick woolen socks, the extra room will be needed." In his other hand was a can of mink oil. "You grease those boots every night, and they will stay dry inside," he told Tyler.

Jack entered last holding out a pair of new red suspenders. "No belt ever completely does the job," he said with a grin, "and no teamster wears anything but red."

At supper that night, Andy Schwanke handed Tyler a knife in a leather sheath. "Made it myself," he said proudly, "Tom helped with the case. You wear it every day. It just might come in handy."

The harnesses were gone over completely, from collar to crupper. The horses had their big feet trimmed and shod, and the pinto had two teeth filed down. They would be taken by train from Eau Claire to Mellen. Tyler would travel with them. He was anxious and excited, wanting his new adventure to begin, but still somewhat sad about leaving the Porters. He promised he would try to be home for Christmas.

"Mr. Nichols said he would close the camp for a week at Christmas," he told Julia, "so I should be home."

Julia hugged Tyler as a mother hugs a child of her own. "Yes," Julia said, "this is your home, and always will be."

CHAPTER NINE

The train whistle blew one long blast as it slowly eased into the station at Mellen at seven in the morning. A stocky blonde-haired man with a big grin was waiting with his hands on his hips. A ramp was rolled up to one of the freight cars, and the door slid open. The stocky blonde man walked over and yelled "anybody in there?"

Tyler stepped into the doorway. "Are you the man Mr. Nichols sent to help me?"

"Yes. I'm Lars Halverson. The boss said to help you get the horses back to camp." Tyler had the horses already harnessed and led them down the ramp. "There's a wagon full of things parked behind the station," Lars said, "we can hitch up the teams and go."

"How far is it to the camp?" Tyler asked.

"It's twelve miles," Lars said, "we should make it in about three hours."

"What's all in the wagon?" Tyler asked as they drove along.

"It's the big kitchen stoves and equipment that was too big for the truck," Lars said, "otherwise, everything is at the camp."

"Are the stables and forge ready?" Tyler asked.

"Mr. Elmer Krause made sure of that," Lars said, "he's Mr. Nichols partner, and he likes horses. He is really anxious to meet you."

"Is the full crew there now?" Tyler asked.

"Right now it's the trail cutters and carpenters," Lars said. "The logging crew should be here next week. Mr. Nichols is getting them together now."

The trail into camp had been roughly graded with a dragline towed behind the truck. It was better than it was, but still needed work.

"Whoa," Tyler hollered as they drew up by the main building.

A man stepped out on the porch with a big smile. "You made good time," he said. "I'm Elmer Krause. I'll have some men unload the wagon." Looking over the horses he said, "Galen told me I would be surprised at the horses. Tell me about them."

"The Suffolks are a fine team, and well trained," Tyler said. "The other team are a white Irish mare and a Pinto gelding. They work separate or as a team, but only with each other."

"My father worked his farm with Irish horses," Elmer said. "I've always been partial to them." Looking around, Elmer yelled, "I need six men to unload this wagon!" Turning to Tyler he said, "Unhitch the horses and take them to the stable. They need a good drink and some feed.

"I'll show you the trail we laid out," Elmer said. "It still might need some work, tell me what you think."

Tyler liked what he saw. "It's wide enough for a team" he said, "and you filled in the low spots with logs."

"There are a few stumps that need to be pulled out," Elmer said pointing them out. "The horses should be able to take care of them."

"I'll need at least one more man who knows horses," Tyler said, "two would be even better."

"The Oleson brothers, Joe and Mike, will be here tomorrow," said Elmer. "Both are in their twenties and have been working with horses since they were boys." On the way back to camp, Elmer asked, "Were you in the war?"

"Was in the 32nd Infantry," Tyler said with pride, "was at the Meuse-Argonne when the war ended."

With a big grin, Elmer said, "Galen and I were in the Marines. We fought on your right flank!" The two men faced each other with a new respect as the memory of the battle passed between them. Elmer held out his hand, and as Tyler clasped it, he said, "I think I'm going to like working here."

Standing in the door of the bunkhouse, Tyler got a good look at how he would live for the next eight months. Two stoves took up the center aisle, about twenty feet apart. Bunk-beds lined the walls, shotgun style. Against the far wall was a long washstand with room for three basins and pitchers and a barrel for water. Lines were strung high all across the room for drying wet clothing. Four benches sat between the stoves. Wood for the stoves would have to be bought in daily. Tyler chose a lower bunk near the door. He and the two other teamsters would be roused by the cook's helper an hour before the rest of the crew. It was their job to have the horses ready to go right after breakfast. Walking to the cookhouse, he opened the door and stepped inside. Four men were finishing setting up setting the new stoves in place. A tall, bulky man with gray hair was giving orders."

"Careful with those stovepipes" he hollered, "turn the damper to the off-side so I can reach it." When he turned, he saw Tyler, and said, "You must be the stable manager. I'm Casper Schultz, the cook."

"Shaking Casper's hand he said, "I'm Tyler Braun, nice to meet you."

"I'll have sandwiches and coffee ready for lunch in a half hour, so take a look around." Long tables took up most of the room, with benches on either side. Pegs lined the log walls to hand coats on, with two large overhead fixtures for lighting. It was a place for men to get a good meal before spending a day cutting trees. A doorway had been cut through the logs on the west side. This led to the office and sleeping quarters Galen and Elmer.

The equipment shed was next. An older man sat on a bench outside using a file to sharpen a two-man saw. The door was open, and Tyler looked inside. Axes, single and double bit stood against one wall, next to the mauls and a box of wedges. Another wall held the saws, and another had shelves for all manner of files and whetstones. Bundles of new axe handles lay on the floor under the one window. Tyler nodded to the man on the bench and continued on to the forge. The bellows was hooked up and the anvil sat on a huge oak stump, ready for the hammer. Boxes of blacksmith tools were open on the floor. Time enough to sort them out later. The stables were clean with straw on the floor. Two sets of double doors would keep it warm enough in the winter. Two large metal bins held oats and bales of hay were stacked against the side of the building. The horses were in the large corral resting. 'They sure did a good job laying this out' thought Tyler. Just then the dinner bell rang. Time for lunch.

The logging crew arrived in two trucks. Galen drove one, Mick Hanlon the other. It was an odd assortment of men who climbed down from the flatbeds. Swedes, Poles, Norwegians Germans and French. Some were tall, some shorter, most stocky built, a few lean, none fat. All were tan and wore boots. It was almost noon when they arrived, and they all were hungry.

"Cooky has sandwiches and coffee for you," Mick told them. "You got a half-hour to eat, then we go to work. It takes a lot of firewood to keep the stoves cooking. Today we make Cooky happy." The men filed into the cookhouse and sat down. There was no talking, just hungry men fueling up for some hard work.

Tyler was watching as the men finished eating and stepped back outside. Two blonde haired young men separated from the group and walked toward the stables.

"You must be the Oleson brothers," Tyler said.

The older of the two held out his hand. "I'm Joe," he said, "and this is my brother Mike."

"I'm Tyler Braun, the stable manager," Tyler told them. "I want one of you to take the Irish and the other the pinto. Use the go-devils and haul the logs up behind the cookhouse. A crew will be waiting to cut and split the wood."

Turning around, he yelled, "Hey Mick, I need one man to help pull stumps." Waving his hand to show he heard, Mick pointed at a man and motioned with his thumb.

The man walked over to Tyler, held out his hand saying, "I'm Carl Kleutsch from Minong. I guess I'm your stump puller."

"Get a shovel and follow me," Tyler said with a grin. The Suffolks were harnessed and ready.

It was interesting, Tyler thought, watching the men pair off as they worked. Where you were from didn't matter, it was the way you swung an axe, or the way you used a saw that decided who worked best together. Tyler watched the Oleson boys as they chained the logs to the go-devils and hauled them out. Both were patient and the horses seemed at ease with them. The stumps were pulled and the holes filled in with rocks and dirt. Mick, carrying an axe, was everywhere. He watched the crew carefully, noting how each man did his job. Knowing his men could mean the difference between life and death if an accident happened. As the logging boss, it was Mick's job to be ready for anything.

At 5am on September 2nd, Mick Hanlon stepped into the bunkhouse, turned on the light and yelled, "You men have got fifteen minutes to get dressed and get to the cookhouse!" The men scrambled from their bunks and got dressed. It was still dark when they filed into the cookhouse to eat. Breakfast was hot oatmeal or cornmeal, biscuits, molasses syrup and coffee. As the men finished eating they moved outside, a few lighting pipes.

As Tyler was leaving, Cooky handed him a paper-wrapped package. "Horses like biscuits too," he said with a smile.

"Thanks Cooky," Tyler said with a grin, "I'll tell them you sent them."

CHAPTER TEN

Within a week, the work slipped into a pattern. The hardwoods were notched, sawn and dropped. The limbs were chopped off and the logs were cut into twelve foot lengths. Using the go-devils, Joe and Mike hauled them to the main trail. Using the team of Suffolks, Tyler could haul three logs at a time out to the loading area where the trucks waited. Using an overhead boom and a chain hoist, the logs were lifted onto the long flatbed trailers. The trucks drove the twelve miles to the railroad siding where four flatbed rail cars waited. Another boom and chain hoist lifted the logs from the trucks to the cars. When all four rail cars were loaded, they were hauled to the mill, and four empty cars were dropped off. "This sure beats waiting for ice-out in the spring" Galen said, "and we get paid by the carload."

By the end of October, a quarter of the tract had been cleared.

"We are ahead of schedule," Elmer told the crew. "This will pay off in January on days when it is too cold to cut."

Lunch was bought out to the crew by truck every day, usually sandwiches and coffee. The big meal came at sundown. Cooky earned his pay with a well-planned menu. Every Sunday morning he served flapjacks, sometimes with bacon. Sunday was a day off for the men, a day to mend torn clothes, darn socks and do laundry.

A huge kettle sat over a fire-ring. The kettle was filled three-quarters with water, and when it was boiling, the clothes went in! The crew took turns stirring the kettle and adding a little soap. The clothes were wrung out and hung to dry in the bunkhouse.

In the evening, Homer Ebert would tune up his fiddle and play. Dieter Groff would follow along on his harmonica. Armond Pontillo had a soothing tenor voice and could often be encouraged to sing. Tyler took this time to write letters. They would be delivered to the train station by the truckers.

"Get out of the way! It's gonna roll!" At the top of his lungs, Mick tried to clear men away from the tree. The big thirty foot oak toppled from the stump, and should have fallen straight down. Instead, it rolled to the left, twisting the top of the tree to the right. All but one man got clear. Ewald Jenner, an axeman, stumbled. As he tried to rise, one of the thick oak branches crashed down on the calf of his right leg, pinning him to the ground. With a final THUMP! The tree settled to the ground. The crew rushed forward with axes to cut the big branch.

"NO!" Mick yelled. "We have to prop the trunk up, otherwise it might roll again!"

It took an hour to cut up another log to use as levers and props. Finally, the crew was able to cut the branch off and drag Ewald from underneath.

Wincing in pain, Ewald said, "I think the leg is broke."

Tyler had been busy chaining two logs to the go-devil.

"Lay him on top of the logs," Tyler said, "I'll take him up to the office and call an ambulance to take him into Mellen."

The two logs were chained together and Ewald was laid on top. Some pine boughs with a coat thrown over supported the leg. Tyler started up the trail slowly. "If we need to stop, you yell out," Tyler told Ewald.

"I'm doing good," Ewald said, "just don't drive under the chain hoist." Tyler grinned, then started laughing, which got Ewald laughing! After that, the ride went easy.

The first snow began drifting down just after midnight on the second Monday in November. By five 0'clock, it was still snowing and the wind had picked up. Mick turned on the light in the bunkhouse and told the crew, "Go get breakfast. When the wind dies down, we cut."

At seven o'clock the snow quit, the wind died off, and the sun shone bright on a five inch cover of pure white. The temperature held steady at 25 degrees as the crew headed into the woods. Tyler and the Oleson boys followed behind. Soon, the sound of saws and axes filled the air as the big hardwoods brought down a shower of snow as each tree fell. The main trail packed down as Tyler hauled the logs out to the waiting trailers. The work went a bit slower as the crew was careful handling the wet timber.

"Clean the snow out of the hooves," Tyler told Joe and Mike. "If it packs in there, the horses will start slipping." By sundown, the trail was packed down. Tired and wet, the men walked slowly back to the bunkhouse.

On Thanksgiving day, the crew worked until noon. Mick had told them, "Work up an appetite, because Cooky has a real treat for you!" As the crew filed into the cookhouse, the aroma of roasting chicken almost overpowered them. The two cooks helpers carried out platters of chicken, a half chicken per man. Then came large bowls of mashed potatoes, tureens of giblet gravy, cooked cranberries, fresh baked bread and coffee. Galen and Elmer had scoured the countryside, buying chickens and potatoes from the local farmers. The men took their time eating, enjoying the feast.

The first week in December, it snowed twice. The first was a light fluffy couple of inches, the second was the storm, with high winds and over a foot of snow. The storm lasted two days, and when it was over, the crew shoveled the drifts from the buildings. Tyler and the Oleson boys opened the trails with the wooden plow. It took a four horse hitch to bust through some of the drifts. The cutting went slow, and dragging the logs out to the main trail took time and patience.

Mick told Tyler, "Only two logs at a time son, and rest the horses when you need to." By sundown, each man knew he had more than earned his days' pay.

CHAPTER ELEVEN

As she rolled out the cookie dough, Julia caught herself humming a Christmas song. In his last letter, Tyler had written he would be at the train station in Eau Claire on the morning of the 21st. Jack had gone to pick him up an hour ago, while Tom and Andy put up the tree in the parlor. Molly lay quietly, watching them.

"Hold it right there," Tom said. Andy held the tree as Tom adjusted the stand. Stepping back, Tom grinned, saying, "This time, it's absolutely straight."

Andy stepped back smiling. "By golly, we did it." Then, they heard the truck coming up the driveway, with Jack honking the horn. Molly ran out the door as Tom opened it, barking in excitement. As Tyler stepped down from the truck, Molly got the first hug, then Tom, then Andy. The smiles on their faces told of their happiness in welcoming him home. Julia stepped out on the porch, wiping her hands on her apron. Tyler ran to the porch steps and hugged her as tears formed in the corners of her eyes. It felt so good to have Tyler home!

In the kitchen, over coffee and cookies, Tyler wanted to hear all that had happened while he was gone. "We sold one pair of Belgians as breeder stock to a man from Iowa,"

Jack said, "and a week later bought two Belgian mares, with papers, at an auction in Illinois."

"This was our best year ever, buying and selling horses," Tom said.

"How is your pet mule working out?" Tyler asked Julia.

"Clapping her hands together and laughing, Julia said, "Little Jenny is so smart, it is a pleasure to work with her, but she does go after those carrot tops."

"And I finally broke down and got electric lights in the forge," Andy said with pride. "Now tell us about life in a lumber camp" Jack said.

Tyler explained the layout of the camp and the daily routine. He told how the Oleson boys, Joe and Mike, cared for the horses. "Joe likes working with the Irish horse and Mike with the Pinto," he said, "and I use the Suffolks to bring the logs to the trailer to be loaded."

"How is the food?" Julia asked.

Smiling, Tyler said, "Cooky is a marvel in his kitchen. We had a Thanksgiving dinner that I will remember a long time." Tyler related the accident that broke Ewald Jenner's leg, and the big storm just a few weeks past. It was getting late and people were yawning.

"Let's get some sleep," Jack said. "Tomorrow we have some decorating to do."

For Tyler, it was like living in a dream. It would be his first Christmas with a family of his own. As he worked with Tom making a large wreath for the front door, He thought back on the Christmases spent in the orphanage. There was always a tree to decorate, packages to wrap and a Christmas dinner. What was missing was a sense of family, the closeness of parents and the feeling of belonging. Mary had been the only really close relationship in his life. How he missed her!

"Now we need a big red bow," Tom said, bringing Tyler back from his memories.

"Julia has one already made," Tyler said, "I'll get it."

With the bow attached, Tom hung the wreath on the door. Putting his arm around Tyler's shoulder, Tom said, "We are all so glad you could make it home, it wouldn't be Christmas without you."

From the attic, Jack bought down two boxes of ornaments and a box of candle holders to clip onto the tree branches. Andy was stringing popcorn to wrap around the tree. Occasionally a popped kernel would drop from his big hands, and Molly was waiting to snap them up.

Julia carefully unwrapped the tissue paper from a winged angel. "Jack, this goes on top of the tree," she said, " and be very careful."

Tom showed Tyler how and where to attach the candle holders. "We light them on Christmas morning," he said, "after we get back from the mass at church."

"Did I smell stollen baking this morning?" Jack asked.

Smiling, Julia said, "I baked two this morning."

"What is stollen?" Tyler asked.

"It's special bread mixed with fruit and nuts," Julia answered. "The recipe came from Germany many years ago."

"My mouth is watering just thinking about it!" Tom said with a grin.

From the box in front of her, Julia lifted out a spun glass ornament. It was painted green and red, and was delicate as a robin's egg. She gently hung it on the tree. Then came the small painted wooden ornaments. Soldiers, snowmen, horses, sleds, and stars. A pine log snapped in the fireplace, and a fine shower of sparks briefly flared. 'Christmas at home' thought Tyler, 'what a wonderful feeling.'

Christmas morning was a ritual in the Porter family. Jack had uncovered the big sleigh kept in the storage shed. A four horse hitch of Belgians would take the Porter's to church. Andy had left early in the truck to make sure the old pipe organ was working properly. The temperature was 35 degrees with no wind. Dressed warmly, Tyler wished the ride would never end.

As they drew near the catholic church, they saw several other sleighs already there, along with numerous autos. People hugged and shook hands with neighbors they had not seen in months. The decorations inside had been done by the Ladies Aide Society. Garlands on the pews, the nativity scene, the candles and the bright red Poinsettia's at the altar. The pipe organ was working fine as Christmas hymns were sang by the choir. The perfect beginning to a special day.

Back home, coffee and hot cider was sipped as the gifts were opened. Julia had been knitting all year, and all the men got hats, mittens and scarves. There were several new aprons for Julia, and a locket with a picture of their daughter from Tom. Jack kept his gifts simple. New wool shirts for the men and a shawl for Julia. Tyler gave wool socks to everyone.

Christmas dinner was a pot roast with carrots, potatoes and onions. Coffee and hot cider were there to wash it down. The stollen was eaten as fast as Julia could cut it. When everyone had eaten as much as they could hold, Jack went into the pantry and returned with a half-full bottle.

"My own homemade blackberry brandy," he said with a smile. He poured a small drink for everyone and said, "A toast, to Julia for the fine meal and to the Porter family assembled here."

Tyler, not used to liquor, took a sip and gasped. With a breathless whisper he said, "Tastes good."

Tom patted his back and, grinning, said, "This is why we only toast once a year. Jack's brandy is tasty, but kicks like a mule."

Taking the train, Tyler made a long overdue visit to Mother Superior Veronica. Holding him at arm's length for a moment she remarked, "Your eyes tell me you have found happiness."

Smiling, Tyler said, "The Porter family has adopted me as one of their own. In a way, their boy Louis came home."

"I am so happy. You deserve to be happy." Mother Veronica then told him the epidemic was almost at an end with no cases reported in three months.

"At the logging camp, we get so busy that we don't keep up with the news," Tyler said. He told her about life in the camp and how he enjoyed the work. On his way home, Tyler promised himself to write the orphanage more often.

CHAPTER TWELVE

Tyler got back to the logging camp on Friday afternoon, January 2nd, 1920. He caught a ride to the camp with a trucker who talked all the way.

"I'll tell you, the country has gone plumb crazy," he said, "they closed all the saloons, and gave the women the right to vote."

"You don't think women should vote?" Tyler asked.

"Things are changing just too fast," the trucker said, "I just don't think the country is ready for it."

Tyler got out at the driveway and went to check on the horses. The Oleson boys had split their time at the stable, and the horses were fine. About one-third of the men were back with the rest arriving all weekend. At the cookhouse, Cooky was dishing out bowls of beef stew. Biscuits and coffee completed the meal. Crawling into his bunk that night, Tyler wished he were still back home at the Porter house.

The spring of 1920 came early. The weather broke in late February, and by the middle of March, the snow was gone and the temperatures never got below 40 degrees at night.

"I seen the same thing happen back in 1886," one old-timer said, "and that summer was a drought."

Only one day of heavy rain kept the crew out of the woods. The cutting went quickly, and by April, the last loads of timber were being loaded on the trailers. Galen and Elmer got the men together on April 7th.

"It is our pleasure to inform all of you that by completing the cutting a month early, you have earned a $25 bonus, each." A cheer went up from the crew, and Mick waved his hand to settle them down. "Get your belongings together," he said, "and right after lunch, line up at the office for your pay."

Like many of the crew had done, Tyler had waited to be paid at the end of cutting. Elmer handed him an envelope and said, "at $75 a month your pay comes to $525. For the great job you did with the horses, your bonus is $75, giving you a total of $600, and you earned every cent."

"Hesitating a moment, Tyler asked "what happens to the horses?" Smiling, Elmer told him "The Oleson boys are buying the Irish and the Pinto. Galen is taking the Suffolks home with him." Two trucks were waiting to take the men to the station in Mellen.

Tyler decided to do some shopping before he took the train home. Downtown Mellen was busy, auto's and trucks competed with horse drawn wagons for the right of way. Seeing the striped pole of a barbershop, Tyler decided a haircut was in order. One man was in the barber chair and one was waiting.

"Be with you in about 10 minutes," the old barber said with a grin. While he waited, Tyler picked up a newspaper from the table. The headline read MURDER IN MILWAUKEE! Reading on, the story told of bootleg whiskey haulers shooting it out with a rival gang. Two men had been killed and one hospitalized, under police custody. "Your turn, young fella," said the barber.

The evening train left at six, with Tyler aboard. Watched from a window seat as twilight cast shadows across the landscape. He reflected on his time at the logging camp and, although it had been something new and exciting, logging was not in his future plans. He wanted to continue working with horses, maybe try riding horses. Although auto's were taking over the roads, the countryside still counted on men on horseback. The porter entered the car and informed the passengers that there would be a one hour stop in Hayward.

'Time for a coffee and maybe a sandwich,' thought Tyler. He asked the station master if there was a cafe open. Checking his watch, the man said, "it's a quarter to nine, Joe's Cafe is still open. It's a half block south." The cafe was just about to close, but Joe, the cook, made him a cold beef sandwich and a coffee. "Leave the cup with the station master," Joe said as he locked the door. When Tyler got back to the station, a small crowd of men wearing badges were escorting two men on board. Tyler asked a young deputy, "What's all the fuss about?"

"We arrested two bank robbers. We will hold them in Eau Claire overnight, then take them to Madison for trial," The deputy said.

"Why is the trial in Madison?" asked Tyler.

"Bank robbery is a federal crime," said the deputy, "the nearest federal court is in Madison." The deputy's name was John Burnell, he was twenty-years-old and had just been appointed deputy two months ago. "I went through six weeks of hard training," John said, "but it pays $150 a month, which is a lot more than I made delivering telegrams."

It was early morning when the train stopped in Eau Claire. Across from the station and down one block was the livery stable. Tyler took a slow walk, breathing in the cool morning air. There were four horses in the corral, two draft horses, an older mare and a gray gelding. Slipping through the corral rails, Tyler approached the gelding to look it over. Stroking it's neck, Tyler lifted its upper lip and checked the teeth. 'Seven, or maybe eight years old. Clean lines, no open sores or scabs, and the eyes are clear.'

"If you like that one, I can make you a good deal," said a voice behind him. Turning around Tyler saw a man of about forty, stout but not fat. He was sipping coffee from a big mug. Tyler walked over and held out his hand.

"I'm Tyler Braun," he said, "are you the owner?"

Shaking Tyler's hand the man answered, "I'm Blaine Dahlquist. I usually get here early to feed the horses before the day begins." Pointing at the gelding he said, "Just took that one in two days ago. The owner died, his wife sold me the horse. He's seven years old, in great condition." Rubbing his chin a moment he said, "I can let him go for fifty dollars, saddle included." Tyler reached down and picked up each hoof in turn.

Rising, he said, "The hooves need trimming and new shoes all around. Forty would be a good price, saddle included."

Grinning , Blaine said, "I like doing business with a man who knows horses. Forty it is."

Headed out of town on horseback, Tyler put the gelding through its paces. The horse had been well trained and was eager to run. It had been almost two years since he had ridden, but the gelding made the ride easy. Farmers waved as Tyler passed by, and when a Model-T honked it's horn and passed him, the horse never broke stride.

Tom and Julia were hanging out rugs and quilts to air out from the winter. Shading his eyes, Tom said, "Someone is coming up the drive on horseback."

Laughing, Julia said, "It's Tyler, I just know it's Tyler."

As he drew nearer, Tyler waved his hat and yelled, "Hello the house!" Andy and Molly appeared from the forge and Jack stepped out on the porch. Tyler stepped down from the gelding, shook Tom's hand. Tyler hugged Julia while Molly pranced around giving out excited yips.

"Where did you get this fine-looking horse?" Jack asked.

"I bought him from Mr. Dahlquist at the livery stable about an hour ago," Tyler answered.

"You still have an eye for good horses," Jack said with a grin, "glad you're back."

CHAPTER THIRTEEN

That evening over supper, the family talked about the changes since the start of the new year. "Horse sales are down," Jack said, "but breeders are still looking for purebred stock for show animals. We now have a fine pair of purebred Friesians, and the vet says the mare is in foal."

"Are you still thinking of phasing out the Percherons?" Tom asked Jack.

"We will always keep a pair of Percherons," Jack said smiling, "in memory of my father."

"Sheriff Patten stopped by yesterday," Julia said. "He says there is someone operating a still in the area, and wants us to keep an eye out for unusual activity."

"I have a bad feeling this prohibition is going to get out of control," Andy said, "if people want alcohol bad enough, someone will supply it."

"Have you registered to vote?" Tyler asked Julia.

"I certainly have," Julia answered, "and I intend to do so at the first opportunity."

Jack and Tyler stood in the morning sunrise at the corral, coffee cups in hand, watching the Friesians. "They were bred in the Netherlands for one purpose only," Jack said. "They are the only horse created just for war, a horse strong enough to carry men in full armor at a gallop.”

“How tall are they?” Tyler asked.

“They both stand 16 hands high,” Jack said, “although their midnight black color make them seem bigger than that.”

“The German cavalry was mounted on Friesians,” Tyler told Jack, “but when they went to trench warfare, they used the horses to haul wagons and cannons.”

Andy came from the forge smiling. “I trimmed and shod the mare yesterday. She stood as meek as a lamb. I expect the same from the stallion today.”

“When will the mare drop her foal?” Tyler asked.

“The vet says it will be in three months,” Jack replied, “if all goes well.”

Just then, Sheriff Jeff Patten’s Ford drove into the yard. Getting out he said, “Good morning Jack, I’m hoping you can help me.”

“Let’s go in the house for coffee,” Jack said, “and you can tell me how I can help.”

Sitting at the kitchen table, the sheriff explained his situation. “Seven miles down the highway from you is the old Fedderspiel farm.”

“I know the place,” Jack said, “it’s been vacant since the old bachelor died in 1915.”

Sipping his coffee, the sheriff said, “Well, last week when I drove by, I noticed fresh tire tracks leading to the old barn. I parked the car and walked in. Someone has a truck parked in there.”

“The bank owns the property,” Julia spoke up, “has it been sold or rented?”

"I checked with Gavin Pringle at the bank," the sheriff said, "and nobody is supposed to be there. I am going to take a closer look, but I need some backup. My deputy is taking a prisoner to Madison today, which leaves me short-handed."

"I'll go with you sheriff," Tyler said, "let's go take a look."

Looking Tyler over carefully, the sheriff said, "You were in the war, weren't you?"

"I was with the 32nd Infantry" Tyler said, "mustered out as a Sergeant."

Standing up, Sheriff Patten told Tyler "Raise your right hand, I'm going to swear you in as a temporary deputy."

The old farmhouse and barn sat on a slight rise about seventy yards from the road. Sheriff Patten walked slowly ahead, his right hand resting on the grip of his .44 caliber single action Colt. Tyler followed a few yards behind and slightly to the sheriff's left, carrying the sheriff's pump action 12-gauge Winchester. Approaching the barn, they looked in through a dusty window. The Old Dodge truck was there.

Moving slowly to the house, they circled around the back, brushing aside the weeds. The back door was closed. Shading his eyes, the sheriff looked through the dirty window. Backing away slowly, he motioned to Tyler to follow.

Standing in the shade beside the porch, the sheriff whispered, "There is a man lying on the sofa. He appears to be sleeping. I am going to try the door." With his left hand the sheriff slowly turned the door knob. It opened with a slight rusty groan. Stepping inside, he motioned Tyler to follow. They were in the kitchen. Moving around an old table, they stepped through an open doorway into the parlor. The man on the sofa was snoring softly. Beside him on the floor was a half-full gallon jug. There were sounds of someone moving around in the basement. Motioning Tyler to stay with the sleeping man, the sheriff walked to the basement door. He drew his pistol and started down.

"Finally woke up, did you Fred," came a loud voice.

"Raise your hands above your head," hollered the sheriff, "I'm Sheriff Jeff Patten and you are under arrest for trespassing!" There was a yell, a sound of breaking glass and a gunshot! The man on the couch began to rise. Tyler pushed the muzzle of the shotgun against the man's chest and pushed him back down. Looking completely confused the man slowly laid back down, stared wide-eyed at Tyler and raised his hands above his head.

There were footsteps on the stairs and another man appeared with his hands raised. The sheriff was right behind him, prodding him along with his pistol in his back.

"You should see the still they built in the basement," the sheriff said with a big smile on his face, "gonna be a pity to bust it up."

"What was the gunshot about?" Tyler asked as they marched the men outside.

"When I told him to raise his hands, he threw a piece of firewood through the basement window," the sheriff said. "When he tried to crawl out, I shot a hole in the ceiling, which changed his mind real quick."

The men were Fred Buelow and Lyman Jacoby, both in their early twenties, and just a month out of Waupun Prison. The men were handcuffed and put in the backseat of the patrol car. "Ride into town with me," Sheriff Jeff said to Tyler. "I believe you may have a career in law enforcement."

"We can sure talk about it," said Tyler, smiling.

Sheriff Patten dropped Tyler off at the Porter house as the sun was setting. Jack and Tom were in the corral working with a Percheron mare. Julia was on the porch knitting, and dropped her half-knitted mitten in the basket. She met the sheriff and Tyler in the yard.

"I think Tyler has the makings of a fine deputy," he told Julia, "he can tell you all about our day over supper tonight."

Tyler filled everyone in on the arrest of the bootleggers. "Neither one was armed," he said. "Not even a pocket knife."

"How long had they been making the whiskey?" Tom asked.

"The sheriff figures from the jugs in the basement, they probably had been cooking mash for over a month," Tyler said. "They would make the whiskey during the day and bring it into Eau Claire to sell at night."

"Has the sheriff talked you into becoming a deputy?" asked Julia.

Thinking a moment, Tyler said, "I would like to try it. It pays $250 a month and I get a patrol car to ride around in."

"How much training do you get?" Jack asked.

"I would have to take a two-week training course at Camp McCoy," Tyler answered, "and the next training group starts Monday."

"Sounds like an interesting job," Andy said.

"Sounds like a dangerous job to me," Julia said softly.

"Enforcing the law can be dangerous," Tom said, "but it can also be rewarding. Protecting your friends and neighbors from those who would do them harm is necessary, and should be done by responsible people. I believe Tyler fits that description."

Clearing his throat, Jack said, "Having fought in and survived a world war, Tyler is aware of the dangers and has already made up his mind, haven't you Tyler?"

Nodding his head, Tyler said, "I will be on the train to Camp McCoy Monday morning."

CHAPTER FOURTEEN

Eau Claire was growing. It had started as a sawmill back in 1850. The Eau Claire and Chippewa rivers converge here, and by 1860 there were more than 25 sawmills operating. After the civil war, the white pine loggers were sending thousands of logs to the mills. Factories sprang up, producing everything from rocking chairs to farm wagons. However, along with the honest businessmen came the get-rich-quick schemers and outright criminals.

When the prohibition bill was enacted in 1920, making 'moonshine' became popular. The large breweries turned to making malted milk and candy bars, the smaller ones just locked up and went out of business. Hundreds of unemployed men now searched for a way to survive. Making illegal whiskey was one way, another was robbery.

Sheriff Jeff Patten had his hands full keeping the peace. His only deputy was 27-year-old Ellis Winfield. Ellis stood six foot tall, with brown hair, brown eyes and a lean build. He had served in the Marine Corps for eight years. After the war he turned to law enforcement, for which he was well-suited.

When the sheriff told Ellis he was hiring another deputy, Ellis smiled and said, "it's about damn time." Ellis was courting Claudia Mancel, who was anxious to set a wedding date. "When things quiet down, we can set a date for the wedding. Until then I am just too busy."

The training at Camp McCoy went quickly. Much of what was taught, Tyler already knew. His skill with the Springfield rifle amazed the instructors as they watched him put holes in the bullseye of a target at 200 yards. He was almost as good with the Colt 1911 semi-automatic pistol. When asked if he would like to be an instructor, Tyler declined.

Tom met Tyler at the train station Sunday afternoon. As they drove home in the truck, Tom asked him how the training went.

"It was almost like being back in the Army," Tyler answered, "but the food was much better."

Laughing, Tom said, "Julia has been cooking up a storm today. In case you forgot, yesterday was your birthday."

"I did forget," Tyler said laughing. "I'll bet Julia made a chocolate cake."

"That will come after the fried chicken and potato salad," Tom said.

"Have you been riding the gelding?" asked Tyler.

"I have a few times," Tom answered, "but mostly Julia has been riding him. Almost every morning she is up early and on horseback."

With a big grin, Tyler said, "That makes me very happy."

It was the perfect early summer day. The outdoor thermometer read 76 degrees, with only a slight breeze to stir the new leaves on the oak tree. The garden was already planted and sprouting. The flowerbeds were beginning to work their magic in color. The birthday party was held outside on the plank picnic table.

"Pass that chicken down here," Jack said, "before Andy eats it all." Andy laughed, waving a drumstick in the air. Baked beans, coleslaw, potato salad and apple cider lined the center of the table as the fried chicken made the rounds.

"Tell us about the training, Tyler," Tom insisted.

"A lot of what they taught us, I already knew," Tyler said, "but the training helped bring it back."

"How many were in the class?" Julia asked.

"There were 25 of us," said Tyler, "and we all got a signed certificate from the Lieutenant Governor when it was over."

Julia left the table, went into the kitchen and returned with a birthday cake. Raising his glass of cider, Jack said, "a toast to our 20 year old deputy!" Everyone drank to the toast, and Tom helped serve the cake.

The Sheriff's office was a half-block west of the courthouse, with a small parking lot in the rear. Tom dropped Tyler off, saying "if you need a ride home, just call."

"I should be getting a patrol car today," Tyler said, "if all goes as planned." Tyler had dressed as he usually did. Laced-up work boots, denim jeans, blue cotton shirt and his favorite short-brimmed Stetson. As he reached for the door handle, the door was opened by Sheriff Jeff. Ellis Winfield was standing next to the sheriff, smiling.

"Welcome aboard Tyler," Jeff said, "meet my other deputy, Ellis Winfield. I have some paperwork for you to sign in my office."

"The sheriff said you were in the Army during the war," Ellis said. "What outfit were you with?"

"I was in the 32nd Infantry" Tyler said. "How about you?"

"I was in the Marines," said Ellis, "we supported your right flank at the Meuse-Argonne."

Thinking for a minute, Tyler asked "Would you happen to know two former Marines named Galen Nichols and Elmer Krause?"

Laughing, Ellis said, "Not only do I know them, Elmer is my cousin! Where did you meet them?"

"With a big wide grin, Tyler said, "I spent this last winter with them at their logging camp near Mellen. I was their horse manager."

The sheriff interrupted them, saying "you two will have plenty of time to exchange stories, right now we have things to do." Moving behind his desk, Sheriff Jeff said, "Tyler, raise your right hand to be sworn in." After this came the signing of four papers, then the sheriff reached into his bottom desk drawer and took out a web belt with a holster attached.

"Your official sidearm is a Colt 1911 .45 caliber semi-automatic. You will also be issued a Winchester 12 gauge pump shotgun." From his top desk drawer, Jeff took out a badge which he handed to Tyler. "Pin this on you shirt, then Ellis will take you around and show you what we do here."

Holding out his hand to shake, Sheriff Jeff said, "Glad to have you with us Tyler."

Three cars sat in the parking lot. A 1919 Chevrolet sedan, a black 1918 Dodge and a gray1917 Nash. "The Chevy is the sheriff's car, I drive the Dodge and just last week the County board approved the purchase of the Nash, which will be your patrol car," Ellis said. The Nash had a few dents in the rear fenders, but the tires were new.

"Today you ride with me," Ellis said. "I'll introduce you to some good folks and point out some not-so-good ones."

Stopping in Grady's Cafe for morning coffee, Ellis introduced Tyler to a newspaper reporter, who promised a write-up in his paper. Two local bankers were next, followed by some Eau Claire businessmen. Carline, the waitress, gave him a wink and a smile with his coffee. When they finished coffee, they got in the patrol car and headed north, out of town.

CHAPTER FIFTEEN

Leo Spencer was seventeen-years-old. He was five foot seven with brown hair and eyes and lean of build. Leo owned two things. A 1915 Indian motorcycle, inherited from his uncle who was killed in the war and a .38 caliber Iver Johnson five shot revolver he had won in a poker game. Leo worked part-time at the Standard gasoline station in Draper, fixing and changing tires. He made just enough to pay his room rent and eat once a day.

Leo hated winter. The snow and ice kept his motorcycle off the road for months. Leo dreamed of California, where he could ride all year. Deciding it was time to leave Wisconsin, Leo used his revolver to rob the Standard station, get on his cycle and leave the small town of Draper. He headed south on highway 70, hoping to make the state line by sundown. Turning on to highway 40, Leo stopped just outside the town of Bruce at a roadside diner. After finishing a meal of meatloaf, mashed potatoes and coffee, he robbed the diner, getting only $19.50. He gassed up the cycle in Chippewa Falls, held up the station, and was bound for Iowa by way of Eau Claire.

Tyler and Ellis talked about the war as they drove. "Why did you leave the marines?" Tyler asked.

With a heavy sigh, Ellis said, "Once the fighting was over, I knew I would be going back to a life of boredom. You know what I mean?"

Tyler nodded his head. "I know exactly what you mean. I think that's why I took the logging job, to keep from getting bored."

Ellis pulled into the gas station about five miles north of Eau Claire. "I keep in touch with the sheriff by telephone as I go along" he said, "in case there is anything we need to check on."

Tyler pointed a motorcycle parked by the front door. "Why park there if you need gas?"

"Maybe for a quick get-away," Ellis said stepping out of the car. Just then, the station door banged open, and a young man ran out and straddled the cycle. Drawing his pistol, Ellis hollered "Police! Get off the bike!" It was a very surprised Leo who looked up to see a man pointing a big pistol at him. With both hands on the handlebars, Leo did the only thing that came to mind. He jumped on the starter. Tyler had also drawn his Colt, and without hesitation shot out the rear tire of the cycle.

BANG!

The Colt .45 is a powerful handgun at close range, powerful enough to dump the cycle over on the ground. As Leo lay there stunned, Ellis dragged him out from under the bike and pinned him to the ground. Holstering his Colt, Ellis pulled out his handcuffs, pulled Leo's hands behind his back and cuffed him.

The owner of the station, Billy Barnes, ran out yelling "That man stole $27.00 from me, and I want it back!" Going through Leo's pants pockets, Ellis found the .38 revolver and a wad of cash. Handing the cash to the station owner, he said, "Count out your money."

Tyler said, "I'll watch him while you call Sheriff Jeff."

Ellis walked into the station, saw the telephone on the wall and called. When the sheriff answered, he sounded excited. "Good thing you called in," the sheriff said, "I want you and Tyler to be on the lookout for an Indian motorcycle. The guy driving it has already held up some gas stations and a diner. Be careful! He is armed!"

"Not anymore he isn't," Ellis said, "we got him handcuffed outside Billy's gas station. We are bringing him in." Hanging up, Ellis and Tyler loaded Leo into the patrol car and drove back to town.

The sheriff was waiting for them when they drove into the parking lot behind the office. Ellis helped Leo out of the patrol car and said, "Nobody got hurt, thanks to Tyler."

Leo was led inside the office and back to the holding cell. "Both of you sit down and write up a report" Jeff said, "and I want details." Turning to Leo he said, "How far did you really expect to get on your joyride?"

Leo stared at the floor, then stared at the wall, and finally looked at the sheriff. "I was going to California" he said, "because I hate winter. I guess that plan is shot to hell. Now what about my motorcycle?"

The sheriff slowly shook his head and said, "We'll bring the cycle here and hold it as evidence for your trial. After that we sell it for junk." Leo dropped his head into his hands and sighed heavily.

Ellis took Claudia to supper at Grady's Cafe that evening. He told her all about the arrest of Leo Spencer. "I was ready to shoot that boy," Ellis said, "but Tyler saved him when he shot the tire on that motorcycle. I didn't see him aim, he just shot, and the tire blew."

"It must have been all that training," Claudia said.

Thinking a moment, Ellis said, "Some men are just naturally good with a firearm. I'm sure Tyler is one of them."

Sensing an opportunity, Claudia said, "Now that you have another deputy, you will have more time for other things, like setting a wedding date."

Ellis's full attention went to cutting up the steak he had ordered.

Tyler told the Porter's about the arrest over supper. "What made you think of shooting the tire?" Tom asked.

"It just seemed logical," Tyler said, "without the motorcycle, the boy had no chance to get away. If he had tried, Ellis would have shot him."

"I just knew that job would be dangerous," Julia said softly.

"You did the right thing," Jack said. "Leo will get to spend a few years in jail instead of eternity in a graveyard."

By the end of the month, Tyler had made friends with several farmers and shop owners. Billy Barnes had been spreading the word about the deputy who could shoot-a-fly-off-a-fencepost. His easy going manner and shy smile infatuated several eligible young women, but for his own reasons, Tyler kept his distance. Ellis soon became close friends with Tyler, as did Sheriff Jeff Patten. Tyler and Jeff were not prepared for the news Ellis gave them one Monday morning in June.

"Claudia and I are getting married," he told them. Laughing, Jeff and Tyler slapped his back and shook his hand.

"Did you propose, or did she?" the sheriff asked.

"I just finally decided it was time to make that pretty gal my wife," Ellis said, blushing.

"Have you set a date?" Tyler asked.

"Claudia and her mother are working on that right now," Ellis said, "but I'm quite sure it will be in September."

CHAPTER SIXTEEN

Whenever he got a Saturday afternoon off, Tyler would saddle the gelding and explore the countryside. Lazy bees drifted in and settled in the clover plants. Robins flitted about gathering food for their young chicks. A doe and two fawns moved like brown shadows at the very edge of the woodlot. Skirting around the trees, Tyler came out on a farm wagon trail. Following it, he came back to the highway near the railroad bridge over the Chippewa River.

Dismounting, Tyler led the gelding to the river to drink. The horse lowered its head, but suddenly gave a surprised snort and took a step back. Looking down, Tyler saw a bare foot poking through the long grass along the bank. Parting the grass and weeds, the body of a man became visible, half in and half out of the water. The left leg without the shoe stuck straight out, the other leg was half in the water. Kneeling down, Tyler knew immediately from the odor that this man was dead, and had been for a while.

Clad in work pants and a cotton shirt, it looked as if the body had been washed up from the river. Mounting the gelding, Tyler rode quickly back to the house to call the sheriff.

Tyler rode with Jack in the truck back to the body. They arrived minutes before the sheriff and Doctor Elam 'Doc' Bristol, the county medical examiner. A tarp was laid on the ground. Tyler and Jack rolled the body onto it.

"What do you think Doc?" the sheriff asked.

"This guy has been in the water a couple of days," Doc said, "Won't know much more until I get his clothes off." Using the tarp, the men laid it in the flatbed truck and tied it down.

"I'm going to make some calls," Sheriff Jeff said, "I'll try to find out if we have anyone reported missing recently."

Pointing at Tyler, Doc said, "I sure am glad you found him before the coyotes did, makes my job easier." With the sheriff leading, they drove to Eau Claire.

"Nobody has been reported missing," Sheriff Jeff told Tyler and Ellis on Monday morning.

"Any word from Doc Bristol?" Tyler asked.

"He is on his way over here now," Jeff said, "I hope he found something to help identify the guy."

Doc Bristol entered the office smiling. "Got some good news and some even better news," he said.

"Give me the good news first," said the sheriff.

"The man drowned," Doc said. "I thoroughly examined the body and found no gunshot wounds, knife wounds or any other wounds. I did find water in his lungs."

"Was he carrying any kind of identification?" Ellis asked.

"He had three dollar bills and some change in his pants pocket," Doc answered. "That was it."

"Now give me the better news," the sheriff said.

"The body had a tattoo on his upper left arm," Doc said

smiling. "It was US NAVY. I took his fingerprints and sent them to the Navy Department in Washington D.C."

"It could take months to hear back from them," Tyler said.

"Exactly," Doc said. "This drowning is no longer our problem. We bury him in the Potter's field and if the Navy ever gets back to you, we put a small marker on his grave."

"What about the next-of-kin?" asked Ellis.

"The Navy takes care of all that," Doc said. The four men went silent for a moment, all thinking the same thing. A sad ending for a veteran, but at least he would get a decent burial.

It was Friday afternoon. Tyler and Ellis were finishing up their daily report when a girl and boy walked into the sheriff's station. She looked to be about 12 or 13 years old, and the boy whose hand she held tightly was maybe 8 years old. Their clothes were ragged and dusty, neither wore shoes. Standing just inside the doorway, the girl said, "I think daddy killed mama."

Ellis dropped to one knee and asked, "What is your name child?"

"I'm Ruthann Koznicky and this is my brother Tim," the girl said. Nodding his head, Ellis looked up at Tyler saying, "Their folks are Bill and Evelyn Koznicky. Their home is five miles west of town. Bill likes to get drunk and beat his wife."

Sheriff Jeff walked in just then, saw the children, and said, "They must have walked into town. Better get out there and check it out."

"Bill worked at the brewery, loading kegs of beer on the delivery wagons." Ellis told Tyler as they drove.

"What does he do now?" Tyler asked.

"He's been working part-time at Kline's sawmill," Ellis said, "otherwise he stays home and drinks." The yard was empty except for an old Model-T. As Ellis stepped from the patrol car, the house door banged open and a big man stepped out. Bill Koznicky stood 6 foot 2 inches tall, had wide shoulders, a broad chest and thick arms. He swayed slightly as he walked slowly into the dirt yard. Ellis and Tyler stood in front of their car, waiting to see what Bill would do.

"What the hell do want here, Winfield?" Bill shouted.

"We are here to check on your wife, Evelyn," Ellis said. "Where is she?"

"She is in the house, sleeping," hollered Bill. "Now get in your car and go!"

"Not until I see for myself she is alright," Ellis said.

With a mean grin, Bill replied, "To do that, you got to get past me." Ellis moved slowly forward and to his left while Tyler moved to his right. Looking right at Tyler, Bill snarled, "when I finish with Winfield, I'm coming after you."

As Ellis got closer, Bill charged him, swinging his big fists. Ellis dropped into a crouch, and as the intended blows went over his head, he landed a hard right fist to Bills stomach and a brutal left fist to his face. Bill went to his knees, stunned by the blows. Tyler moved in with his gun drawn and smacked Bill behind his left ear. Bill sank to the ground, out cold. Ellis handcuffed Bill, looked up at Tyler and said, "We make a pretty good team."

Entering the house, Ellis found Evelyn laying across the bed. He checked for a pulse and found none. From the old crank phone on the wall, Ellis called the sheriff. "Bill is handcuffed and Evelyn is dead," he said, "Send an ambulance out to pick her up."

Ellis walked out of the house and told Tyler "Evelyn is dead. This time he broke her neck." Bill was groaning as he drew himself to his knees.

Dropping to one knee, Ellis looked Bill in the face, saying, "This time you killed her. She will suffer at your hands no more." They got Bill to his feet and put him in the back of the patrol car. The ambulance drove into the yard and a young man got out.

"I'm Doctor Kennedy," he said. "Where is the patient." Ellis took the young doctor into the house, back to the bedroom. Feeling for a pulse, he said, "This woman is dead."

"Bill broke her neck" Ellis said. Feeling at the base of her skull, the doctor nodded. "Let's get her back to town."

When Evelyn was loaded and the ambulance was driving away, Tyler and Ellis got back in their patrol car. Bill was moving around in the backseat, straining against his handcuffs.

Turning in his seat, Tyler said, "Sit back and be quiet."

Spitting out his words in anger Bill said, "I'm gonna get out of these cuffs and come after you."

Tyler drew his pistol, leveled it over the seat and quietly said, "I almost hope you do." Something in Tyler's eyes made Bill stop, settle back and stare out the window all the way back to Eau Claire.

Tyler got home late that night. Julia had kept a plate of food warm for him in the oven. Telling the Porters about Evelyn Koznicky was not easy, but Tyler felt it was necessary.

"What will happen to the children?" Julia asked.

"The court will try to find relatives," Jack said, "but I don't think there are any."

"They will probably end up in the county home for children," Tom said.

"I have a better idea," Tyler said. "Tomorrow I'm going to see Mother Superior Veronica and ask a favor."

CHAPTER SEVENTEEN

The children had spent the night with Sheriff Jeff and his wife, Brenda. Jeff was already in the office when Tyler entered the next morning.

"How are the kids doing?" Tyler asked.

"They aren't talking much," Jeff said, "but they are eating just fine. Brenda will get them some clothes today, then we will take them to the county home."

"I want you to hold off on that for a few days," Tyler said, "until I can talk to Mother Superior Veronica in Madison. When I tell her what happened, I know she will want to take them in."

"That sure would be better for them if she did," Jeff said, "but the circuit Judge would have to approve."

"I'm taking the 9 o'clock train" Tyler said. "I'll be back as soon as I can."

Tyler arrived in Madison at noon and went straight to the orphanage. After telling Mother Veronica the problem, she smiled and said, "The Judge who would handle this case is Terrance Prochnow. Terrance and I have worked together before. I am sure he would agree to have the children come here."

The relief showed in Tyler's eyes. "How soon can I bring them here?" he asked.

"Bring them tomorrow," Mother Veronica told him. "I'll call the judge and let him know the children are being cared for."

"Can you tell me how it all happened?" the sheriff asked Ruthann. They were sitting in the sheriff's office while a secretary wrote down the girl's statement. "Daddy was drinking and he told mama he wanted some food to eat." Ruthann looked down at her feet, then looked up and continued. "Mama told him there was no food, then daddy yelled at her and hit her. Mama fell down and hit her head on the corner of the table." A tiny tear came from her eye and slid slowly down her cheek. "Daddy yelled at mama to get up, but she didn't move. Then Daddy picked her up and took her to the bedroom and laid her on the bed, then he closed the door." There were tears in both eyes as she said, "I knew mama was hurt real bad, so I took Tim's hand and we left the house and walked into town."

The secretary had tears in her eyes as she rose and left the office. Ellis entered the room, took Ruthann in his arms and held her as she cried.

"I'll take her back to your house now," Ellis said, "Did you want to talk to Tim?"

With a heavy sigh, Jeff said, "No, I think the Judge will be satisfied with what we have."

"I don't remember," was all Bill Koznicky had to say.

"If you plead guilty, there won't be any need for a trial," the sheriff told Bill. "Either way, you're gonna put me in prison"

Bill said, "So tell the judge I'll plead guilty, but I just don't remember."

"You haven't asked about your children," said Jeff.

"I guess they will go to the county home," Bill said, "probably have it better there than they did at home."

"Evelyn's funeral is tomorrow," said Jeff. "Ellis will take you there in handcuffs." Bill hung his head and nodded.

Ruthann and Tim said goodbye to Evelyn at the church, then Tyler took them to the station and boarded the train. "Where are we going?" asked Ruthann.

Holding her hand, Tyler said, "You are going to live with a wonderful lady in Madison who will love and care for you. This lady works for God so she wears a black dress and goes to church every day."

"Will we ever see daddy again?" Ruthann asked.

"When you want to visit your daddy, Mother Veronica will arrange it." Tim was shaking his head no.

Ruthann said, "We don't want to see him, that's why I asked."

Tim nodded off to sleep with the motion of the train. "Can we go to school at this new home?" Ruthann asked.

"I went to school there," Tyler said. "The teachers are very nice. You will have three meals a day, nice clothes to wear and your own bed to sleep in."

For the first time since he had met her, Ruthann smiled. "It sounds like a wonderful place," she said.

At a brief court appearance, Bill Koznicky stood before Judge Carson Delaney. "This is the third time you have been in my courtroom," said the Judge. "Once for drunk and disorderly, then for assault, in which you beat your wife. She spent three days in the hospital as a result. I then sentenced you to a month in jail and warned you that if this occurred again, I would show you no mercy." Bill hung his head but said nothing. The judge paused a moment, then said, "For the deliberate murder of your wife Evelyn, I sentence you to life in prison. Court dismissed."

Tyler got home late that night, and related his trip to Madison. "The children will be taken care of now," he said with a sigh.

"The judge gave Bill life in prison," Tom said. "Ellis will be taking him to Waupun tomorrow."

Julia set a bowl of chicken soup and a plate of biscuits in front of Tyler. As Tyler ate, Jack asked, "How did the children take to Mother Veronica?"

Smiling, Tyler said, "They were all three smiling and hugging when I left, so I guess this whole thing was sad and cruel, but had a happy ending."

CHAPTER EIGHTEEN

Tyler awoke to someone shaking his foot. "Time to get out of bed," Jack said, "coffee is ready."

"What time is it?" Tyler asked as he yawned.

"It's 5 o'clock, time to go fishing." Jack had two passions, horses and fishing. His knowledge of what was biting and where amazed Tyler, it was like some kind of compass in Jack's head that was seldom wrong.

Tyler got dressed and went to the kitchen where Jack was filling a thermos with coffee. An already filled water jug sat on the table next to a paper bag half full of sandwiches and apples.

"Which lake are we going to today," Tyler asked.

"Half-moon lake," Jack said, "they got panfish as big as a dinner plate and bass as big as muskies."

A half hour drive, just as the sun was coming up, and Jack pulled into a small grocery store and boat rental on Half-moon lake. A stout grey-haired woman came out of the store. "Jack Porter, you old horse wrangler, It's good to see you," she said with a big smile.

"Good to see you too Millie" Jack said. "Is Abner around?"

"He's out back painting a boat. You go in the store, and I'll tell him you're here."

Walking into the store, Jack told Tyler "Abner and Millie Goodey camped here on their honeymoon, and never left. They have been here since 1875. Abner built the store and the boats, Millie handles the money and runs the store."

"The sunfish are biting like crazy, so I knew you would be around soon," Abner said as he entered the store. Abner was 5 foot 10 inches tall with a shock of salt and pepper hair poking out from under his beat up straw hat.

As they shook hands, Jack said, "I want you both to meet Tyler Braun. He served with Louis in the war, now he works with me."

"Pleasure to meet you son," Abner said. "Ready to catch some fish?"

Smiling, Tyler said, "Any day on the water is a good day."

"Well, get your poles and bait and let's get you in a boat." As Jack and Tyler carried their gear to the boat, Abner fetched the oars from the shed. "What are you using for bait?" he asked.

"Grubs and red worms," said Jack.

"Bass will hit on those grubs," Abner said with a little laugh.

Jack rowed out slowly, enjoying the sun on his shoulders. Tyler unwrapped the fishing lines from the long cane poles and set the short handled net to one side. Jack stopped the boat just outside a small bay. "One of the feeder creeks empties in here," he said. "Set your bobber at about three feet and try the red worms."

In an hours' time, they caught six keepers. Three sunfish, two bluegill and a big perch. All went into the wire basket hanging off the side of the boat. The next stop was a lily-pad bed.

"This must be where the bass as big as muskies hang out," Tyler said with a big grin.

"Use the grubs this time," Jack said with a smile. Tyler baited, cast his line and as the bobber hit the water, it went under with a splash! The line went taught, almost jerking the pole from Tyler's hands.

"I got one!" Tyler hollered.

"It's a big one too," Jack said. "Play him a bit, let him get tired out." Jack reached over and got the net, ready to bring the fish in. The fish tried to swim under the boat, then changed direction back to the lily-pads. Tyler kept the line tight and finally was able to bring the fish alongside the boat where Jack slipped the net under it and lifted it into the boat.

"You were not lying," Tyler gasped, "it's huge!" The bass was 15 inches long and weighed almost six pounds. They fished the pads for an hour, catching four more bass, the smallest weighing around three pounds.

"Now I'm going to take you where the big sunfish beds are."

"I have fished before, but never caught this many or this big," Tyler said.

With a sad smile Jack said, "Louis and I used to come here every year since he was six years old."

"I'll bet he is looking down from heaven right now and laughing his wings off," Tyler said.

"I'll bet your absolutely right," Jack said with a laugh.

By noon, Jack and Tyler had their wire basket full of fish, and rowed back. Abner met them and helped pull the boat up on shore. Jack needed both hands to hold up the wire basket.

"Looks like you guys had a fun morning," Abner said.

"We sure did," Tyler said. "I caught the biggest bass I ever saw, and on the first cast!"

"I'll help you get this gear up to your truck, then Millie has some lunch for you."

They ate outside at a picnic table. Millie had made cold roast beef sandwiches and a macaroni salad. Abner came out of the house with four bottles of Molson beer. Jack looked at Tyler who winked back at him. Smiling, Jack said, "Tyler only helps with the horses part time. The rest of the time he is a deputy sheriff for Eau Claire."

Abner set the beer on the table. "My old and dear friend Wally Barkowski lives in Superior, he works the ore boats. Twice a year, spring and fall, he comes to fish." Looking at Tyler he continued. "On each visit, he brings me a case of this good Canadian beer."

Taking a sip, Tyler said. "This is good beer. I'll be back in the fall for some muskies." Abner, Millie and Jack broke out laughing.

Later, Jack left some of the panfish for the old couple. "Have a fish fry tonight," he told them. Tyler knew that he and Tom would spend the afternoon gutting and cleaning fish for their own fish fry.

"Just stand still and let the man work," Claudia said. Ellis was being fitted for a proper suit for their wedding. The coat fit alright, but the pants needed cuffs. The wedding wasn't for a month, but Claudia and her mother wanted everything just right. Ellis liked his future mother-in-law, June, but she tended to be somewhat bossy. When she got under his skin, he'd give her his best 'don't -push-it' look and she would back down.

"I'm on my lunch break," Ellis said. "I have to be back to work in 15 minutes, and I haven't eaten yet."

Clearing his throat, the tailor said, "I'm all done sir. You can put your other pants on now."

On his way back to the office, Ellis bought a sandwich at the cafe and ate it as he walked. He wanted to marry Claudia, he really did, but he would have to speak to her about her mother. Stopping at the corner, he waited for the traffic to thin out so he could cross the street. Four big trucks passed him by, and he noticed all had Minnesota license plates. The loads were covered with canvas tarps, tied down tight. 'whiskey from Canada' he thought, 'headed for Chicago.'

"The Canadian's load the Minnesota trucks at either Grand Portage or International Falls," Sheriff Patten said, "then two men take turns driving, stopping only for gas and food. Their favorite crossing into Wisconsin is at Prescott, then they drive to Beloit and enter Illinois. Almost a straight shot from there to Chicago."

"Why doesn't the Government do something about it?" Ellis asked.

With a heavy sigh, the sheriff replied, "Because the crooks have more men, more trucks and more guns than the feds do. Out of every ten convoys of trucks, the feds maybe get one."

"This whole prohibition law is a nightmare," Ellis said.

"You can thank the Women's Temperance League," the sheriff said with a smirk, "and your new mother-in-law is a flag waving member."

CHAPTER NINETEEN

The Eau Claire Country Club was hosting their fourth annual Midwest golf championship weekend. Thirty top golfers from the neighboring states would be competing for the three foot tall trophy and a thousand dollar prize. It was a big event for the city and bought in spectators from as far away as Kansas City and Memphis. This year would be different. This year, no beer or whiskey would be served due to the prohibition laws.

The Mayor, Chester Dewhurst, called a meeting of the town board to discuss the situation. Sheriff Patten was there, along with Abigail Renford, President of the Women's Temperance League and the manager of the Country Club, Bertram Hamm. The meeting centered around one issue. When the winner of the tournament was presented with the check and the trophy, a bottle of champagne was uncorked and a lengthy toast was given by the Mayor.

"It is a tradition," Chester stated, "and one that must be observed."

"It's alcohol," said Abigail, "and must not be allowed."

"It will only be one bottle," Bertram replied. "Let's ask the sheriff," Chester said.

Jeff stood. "The law states that the liquor must be confiscated, and the supplier to be charged and jailed."

"There must be some middle ground we can agree on," Bertram pleaded. At this point, a voice from the back of the room spoke up.

"I believe I have a solution to your problem." All heads turned as Francine Pringle, the library director rose, and addressed the assembly. Francine was somewhere in her late sixties and had been the director of the library for as long as any of them could remember. She was medium height, gray haired and slender. A strong wind could have blown her away, but her voice held the authority of one used to being in charge.

"I have recently been reading of a man in California who has been experimenting with carbonation," she said. "This man owns several vineyards and now can only produce grape juice. He has been carbonating the juice and selling it as non-alcoholic champagne." Reaching into her purse she produced an envelope, which she handed to Bertram Hamm. "All the information you need is there, along with a price list." For once, both Chester and Abigail were both speechless. In the end, it was decided this would appease everyone and the meeting was dismissed.

The tournament was a success, the winner of the money and the trophy was Henry Bennett, a pro golfer from Elgin, Illinois. Two bootleggers were arrested by Ellis in the parking lot. The men had argued, then began fighting over their split of the profits. They were jailed for drunk and disorderly conduct. A new Pierce Arrow was stolen, the sheriff's department was still looking for it. Otherwise the spectators were orderly and sober. The city merchants had prospered, along with the cafes and restaurants. The two hotels did well, as did the Ford dealership who rented out some used auto's. The hope was that in future years the event would grow and prohibition would end.

Jonas Hauser was dog-tired of farming. His folks, Harry and Lucille Hauser owned the farm, and hoped one day to pass it on to Jonas and his younger brother Frank. Their cousin Donny lived with them. Donny's parents had died during the flu epidemic, and he had come to live with his only other relatives.

Jonas was a veteran of the great war and was a hero to Frank and Donny, both seventeen years old. Jonas liked to tell about the fun he had in Paris before being shipped home. The wine flowed freely, the jazz music was wonderful and the women were very friendly. 'The daily grind of farming is not for me' thought Jonas. But the lifestyle Jonas craved required money, lots of money, which farming would never produce.

Jonas had brought three things back from the war. His uniform, a Springfield rifle, and a Luger pistol he had taken from a dead German Officer. "With the golf tournament over, the bank is just stuffed with money," Jonas told Frank and Donny. "The only way off this farm is to steal a car, rob the bank and drive to Milwaukee."

"Where do we steal a car from?" Donny asked.

Smiling, Jonas said, "I already got the car, I stole a Pierce Arrow from the lot Saturday night when everybody was celebrating. I got it hid in the brush down by the river."

"We only got one gun," Frank said, "that Luger of yours."

"The Pierce Arrow had a .38 Colt pistol in the glove box," Jonas said, "so we got two, which is all we need."

Jonas decided that Donny would drive. He would wait outside the bank with the motor running. He was very nervous, but willing. Jonas and Frank entered the bank on Wednesday afternoon about three o'clock.

"Tellers, raise your hands, everybody else, down on the floor!" Jonas yelled. There were four customers, and they laid down. Frank stood over them holding his pistol. Jonas ran to the first teller, pulling a cloth bag from his pocket.

"Fill this up, and hurry," Jonas ordered. The first teller emptied his register into the bag, then passed it to the second teller, who did the same.

Steven Boyer, the 62 year old bank manager, was watching all this from his office. Quietly, he took a .38 caliber Smith & Wesson from his desk drawer. With a shaking hand, he pointed the gun and shot, hitting Frank in the left arm. Frank screamed, dropped his pistol and ran for the door. Jonas turned, shot Boyer in the chest and ran for the door.

Donny heard two shots, BANG! BANG!, and saw Frank run out of the bank holding his arm. As Frank got to the car and opened the door, Jonas came running out with the bag of money. He pushed Frank into the backseat, then got into the passenger seat yelling at Donny, "Drive, dammit, drive!" Donny took off down Main Street headed east out of town.

Tyler and Ellis had been in Ellis's patrol car, looking for the stolen Pierce Arrow. An auto sped past them in the other lane, weaving slightly.

"That's it!" Tyler yelled, "That's the car we are looking for!"

Ellis hit the brakes, spun around in the road, and took out after the speeding car. They were gaining on it when a man stuck his arm out the passenger window and fired a shot!

Ellis backed off slightly and told Tyler, "See if you can shoot out a rear tire." Tyler leveled his .45 and fired.

BANG!

The car weaved across into the other lane, then back again. Tyler tried again.

BANG!

This time the tire blew out. The Pierce Arrow slewed sideways, slid across the road and went motor first into the ditch. The driver threw open the door, rolled out and crawled away screaming, "Don't shoot me! Please don't shoot me! I ain't got a gun!"

The passenger door opened and a man came out shooting. Tyler shot back, hitting him in the leg. The man fell, shouting in pain. As he raised his pistol again, Ellis shot him in the chest. The man jerked, rolled over and went limp.

Slowly, Tyler and Ellis approached the Pierce Arrow. The driver was laying on the ground with both hands above his head sobbing softly. Ellis checked the body of the man he had shot as Tyler looked in the car. Frank lay on the floor, Blood seeping from his arm and a gash in his forehead.

"Can you walk?" Tyler asked. Nodding his head, Frank crawled from the car and stood.

"This one is dead," Ellis said, standing over the body of Jonas, who lay face down. After checking Frank for a weapon, Tyler tied a handkerchief around his arm and handcuffed him. Ellis got the driver off the ground and put cuffs on him.

"Who is the dead man?" Tyler asked.

"That's my brother, Jonas Hauser," Frank said.

"Oh, my God, it can't be," Tyler whispered in disbelief. With a puzzled look, Ellis asked

"Do you know him?" Taking small steps, fearing his knees might give out, Tyler walked over to the body on the ground, knelt down and slowly rolled it over. Jonas Hauser looked peaceful in death, all his earthly worries behind him. "Take those two back to the sheriff," he told Ellis, "I'll wait for the ambulance and a tow truck."

"What about the money?" Donny asked.

"What money are you talking about?" asked Ellis.

"He means the money from the bank we robbed," Frank said.

"It's on the floor in the front," Donny told him. The passenger door to the Arrow was hanging open. Ellis looked in and saw the cloth bag on the floor. He picked it up and looked inside.

"Well, I'll be damned!" he said. "Hey Tyler, we got some bank robbers here!"

Tyler looked up from the body of Jonas Hauser. "No wonder they were willing to shoot it out with us," he said. Now it makes sense. A stolen car isn't worth getting killed for, but a bank robbery might be."

Ellis put Frank and Donny in the back of his patrol car and headed back to town.

"Two crimes solved in one day," the sheriff said smiling, "that might be a record."

"I never expected Jonas would do something like this," Ellis said, "he was always a daredevil kid, but never really mean or cruel."

Softly, Tyler said, "Jonas was with Louis and me at the Marne River. We fought side by side as the Germans jumped out of those boats, shooting."

Laying his hand on Tyler's shoulder, Ellis said, "If we had not shot him, he might have killed us both, trying to get away."

Someone was pounding on the door, yelling, "I'm from the newspaper, tell me what happened!"

Sheriff Jeff jumped to his feet, yanked open the door and pushed the reporter back. "You will get your story when my report is finished, not before, not go back to your paper!"

The newspaper wasted no time getting the story out. BANK ROBBER KILLED IN GUN BATTLE WITH DEPUTIES! Was the headline. Julia was reading the paper when Tyler got home. She dropped it on the table, rose slowly, and gave Tyler a gentle hug. Tom, Jack and Andy were all there.

Jack said, "Louis and Jonas were friends since first grade. Louis joined the Army first, then a few months later Jonas signed up. Such a terrible end for a young man."

"The bank manager's wife, Edna, is now a widow," Julia added. "She told me last week that Steven was planning on retiring in the spring."

"Those two boys, Frank and Donny, will now be going to prison for twenty years, thanks to Jonas," Tom said sadly.

"But don't forget, the bank got all the money back, thanks to Tyler and Ellis," Andy said.

"I think I need to take some time off and think all this through," Tyler said. "Sheriff Jeff asked me if I wanted to, and I think I will."

CHAPTER TWENTY

"How long do you plan to be gone?" Sheriff Jeff asked Tyler.

"A week, maybe two. I just need to do some thinking."

"Just so you get back for my wedding," Ellis said, "after all, you're my best man."

"Don't worry," Tyler said smiling, "I'll be there."

"You're going to need some transportation," Jeff said, "I wish I could let you take your patrol car, but that isn't allowed."

"I've got an idea," Ellis said. "When Leo Spencer went to prison, he signed his motorcycle over to us to pay for his keep. It's sitting out back, covered with a tarp. Have the garage put a new tire on the back and take that."

"I'll call the garage and have them pick it up today," said the sheriff.

"I think I might like that," Tyler said with a grin.

Tyler, Julia and Jack were sitting around the kitchen table with a map spread out. "Right here on Highway 48 is the small town of McKinley," Jack said, "you go northwest about two miles to Milkweed road."

"Is there a sign?" Tyler asked.

Smiling, Jack said, "The sign is nailed to a big oak tree."

"I should write all this down," Tyler said.

"At the end of the road is Sugar Lake," Jack continued, "they have a small lodge and three cabins they rent out."

"When was the last time you were there?" Julia asked Jack.

Scratching his head a bit, Jack said, "It's been about four years. I took Louis there for his fifteenth birthday."

"Was the fishing good?" Tyler asked.

Grinning, Jack said, "As I remember, we caught bass as big as muskies."

"Take the map with you" Julia said, "at least you will find McKinley."

Tyler packed light. Two changes of jeans and shirts, underwear and socks. A towel. Soap and razor were added. It all fit in his army backpack. His short brimmed Stetson went on top, he didn't want to lose that. He would need goggles, but those he could buy in town.

Julia entered as Tyler was packing, and handed him two handkerchiefs. "Men never think of these until it's too late," she said. "Keep one in your back pocket."

"You be sure and ride that gelding for me," Tyler said, "he needs the exercise."

Smiling, Julia said, "Sometimes, I think you bought that horse for me."

Giving Julia a hug, Tyler said, "If that makes you happy, keep thinking it."

When Tyler dropped off the patrol car, the motorcycle was parked by the back door, ready to go. Sheriff Jeff handed him a new pair of goggles. "Call in once in a while," he said, "let us know how you are doing."

"If the lodge has a telephone, I'll call when I get there," Tyler told him. Tyler slipped on the goggles, jumped on the kick start, and eased out of the parking lot.

'This is a lot like riding a horse,' thought Tyler as he sped along. It was a hot day, with a touch of humidity. The traffic was light, just a few trucks and some tractors. By noon, Tyler drove into McKinley. He gassed up at the Standard station and headed northwest out of town. He saw the sign for Milkweed Road, and another sign under it read SUGAR LAKE LODGE 2 MILES.

The gravel road was wide enough for two cars and in good shape. The tall oaks, maples and birch trees shook their leaves as he drove by. The road ended at a large open area with the log lodge on a slight rise. Below, the calm waters of Sugar Lake spread out. To his right were three log cabins, two had cars parked out front, to his left a framed storage shed.

Parking by the lodge, Tyler eased off the cycle and took off the goggles and his backpack. Carrying the pack, he stepped up to the screen door and entered. To his right was a dining area with five tables and a counter. To his left, a stairway led to a second floor balcony. Straight ahead was the registration desk. Behind the desk sat an older man dressed in a white shirt and suspenders. Removing his glasses, the man smiled and said, "Welcome to Sugar lake Lodge, my name is George Dixon, how can I help you?"

"How much for a cabin?" Tyler asked.

"I have one cabin available," George said, "the rate is $5 per day or $25 a week, that includes meals and boat rental."

"I'll take it for a week," Tyler said. "What time is supper?"

"We start serving at six o'clock," George said. "If you would fill out this card, I'll let my wife Alma know we have another guest. She does the cooking."

Tyler got the cabin nearest the lodge. It was one room with a small bathroom curtained off. A small table with two chairs, a dresser and a double bed near an open window was all the furniture. Pulling his pocket watch out, Tyler saw it was almost 2 o'clock. He set the backpack on the bed and walked down to the lake. Two men were out fishing in a boat. Farther down the beach, a man sat at an easel, drawing on a large pad. Tyler walked up to him and watched the man drawing the shoreline of the lake.

The man turned and smiled. "When I am satisfied with the drawing, I will paint the picture."

"It's really good," Tyler said. "Is it your hobby?"

"It started as a hobby," the man said. "Now a friend in Milwaukee sells them in his shop." Holding out his hand the man said, "My name is Theodore Boehm, call me Ted."

"I'm Tyler Braun, nice to meet you."

"Are you staying long?" Ted asked."

"Maybe just a week. Depends on the fishing."

Ted smiled. "If you want to know the best fishing spots, talk to Audrey. She is the waitress and general handyman around here."

"I'll do that. Right now I think I'll take a nap. It's been a long ride."

Tyler woke to the ringing of a large bell. 'Must be supper time,' he thought. He splashed some water on his face, hand combed his hair and walked to the lodge. As he stepped in, he saw Ted waving him over to his table.

"Please join me," he said, "I would enjoy the company."

Tyler sat down. "What's on the menu tonight?"

With a chuckle, Ted said, "It's probably fish again, but Alma is a good cook." Then Tyler got his first look at Audrey. She was a slender girl of medium height with shoulder length black hair drawn back in a ponytail. Her hazel eyes peeked out from long dark lashes. She was tanned with a light spattering of freckles across her nose.

Smiling, she said, "Who's your new friend Ted?"

"Audrey, this is Tyler, he just arrived today. Tyler, meet Audrey."

"That must be your motorcycle I saw out front," Audrey said, "I've never been on one, but I hear they are fun to ride."

"I'll be here for a week," Tyler said. "I'll be glad to give you a ride."

"He is also looking for some good fishing spots," Ted said.

"You give me a ride, and I'll be your guide," Audrey said with a laugh.

"Are we having fish again tonight?" Ted asked.

"Fried bluegill with a baked potato and buttermilk biscuits," Audrey replied, "and your choice of apple cider or coffee."

"Coffee for me," Tyler said.

"Cider is my choice," Ted answered. Over supper, the two became friends.

CHAPTER TWENTY-ONE

"This is my third year coming here," Ted told Tyler.

"Are you on a vacation?" Tyler asked.

Ted paused a moment. "I'm actually retired from banking. My wife Alice died from cancer four years ago. Since then I travel and paint."

"Where do your travels take you?"

"When the leaves start turning color, I take the train to a small town in New Hampshire. I get a room at a local inn and capture the colors on canvas." Ted paused for a sip of cider. "When it gets to be November, I move on down the coast to Florida. There I stay with friends and do sea pictures and old lighthouses."

"Your paintings must be in demand," Tyler said.

"Yes they are," Ted said with a sigh, "but at times I wish Alice were still with me."

Audrey came to collect their plates and asked Tyler, "Would you like to go fishing after breakfast tomorrow?"

"I sure would," Tyler said, "but I will need a fishing pole."

"I've got some spares. I can loan you one," Audrey said with a smile. Tyler felt like a dim light had been turned on in his chest. It took him by surprise and he blushed slightly. He watched Audrey walk away, and wished she had stayed and talked.

Ted noticed Tyler's blush, and a wistful smile crossed his face. 'I may be witnessing the beginning of a young love,' he thought.

The breakfast bell rang at six am. Tyler was already up and ready for the day. He joined Ted at the table and saw two men from cabin 2 seated and talking.

"Have you met those two?" Tyler asked.

"Yes I have," Ted said, "they are brothers, Carl and Jacob Doberstein from Beloit. Carl owns a bakery, and Jacob owns two dry-cleaning stores. They are both bachelors and avid fishermen."

Audrey took the brothers order, then walked to Tyler's table. "Good morning, you have a choice of oatmeal or pancakes," she said with a smile. They both ordered pancakes and coffee. As Audrey turned to leave, she looked back and said, "As soon as I finish doing the dishes, I'll take you where the fish are biting."

Tyler grinned, "If I help you with the dishes, we could get started sooner."

With a smile and a wink, Audrey said, "You got a deal Tyler."

Tyler's heart did a light flip in his chest.

Ted was grinning. "I think Audrey likes you."

Tyler felt himself blushing and said, "I hope so Ted, because I sure like her."

By 7:30 the boat was loaded with oars, poles, bait, a net

and a wire basket. Audrey wore jeans, a cotton shirt and a straw hat. "Let's go where the bass are hitting," Audrey said as she pointed to her left. "There is a weed bed where they should be feeding right now." Tyler rowed slowly, watching Audrey roll the silk line off the poles. The tip of her tongue poked out from the corner of her lips as she concentrated on adjusting the bobbers and baiting the hooks.

"This is good, right here," she said as she eased the anchor into the water. She handed Tyler a pole and with an underhand flip, dropped her line in the water.

Before Tyler could wet his line, there was a SPLASH! "Got one," hollered Audrey, "get the net ready!" Within a minute, Tyler netted a bass at least three pounds. Laughing, Audrey said, "now it's your turn."

Tyler's line tightened just seconds after it hit the water, the bamboo pole bending almost double as the line raced across the water. "I am pulling up the anchor," yelled Audrey, "in case this one tries to go under the boat."

It took all of Tyler's strength to hold onto the pole as the fish fought. Finally, Audrey was able to get the net under it and bring it in. It took both her hands to hold the bass up. She had lost the straw hat in the struggle, and the light breeze ruffled her dark hair.

"This bass will go five pounds or more," Audrey said, "now guess what we are having for supper!" They were both laughing as the big bass went into the basket.

"Just beautiful" Audrey said.

Tyler could not take his eyes off of her. "Yes," he said. "Just beautiful." Within an hour they caught three more bass and several sunfish.

"What time is it?" Audrey asked.

Checking his pocket watch, Tyler said, "About nine."

"We gotta get back," Audrey said, "I've got things to do today."

"What things?" Tyler asked.

"I've got cabins to clean, beds to make, floors to mop and some windows to wash," Audrey said.

"After I clean these fish," Tyler said, "I'll start on the windows."

"But you are here to relax and have a good time," Audrey said.

Looking into her hazel eyes, Tyler said, "I would rather spend time getting to know you." Tyler could see her blush, even under her tan.

"I think I would like to know you better too," Audrey said softly. They were both quiet as Tyler rowed back to shore.

Ted had his easel set up and was preparing his canvas as Tyler and Audrey beached the boat and got out. He noticed that both were slightly blushing and a little nervous.

"Are you going to start painting today?" Tyler asked.

"The drawing is complete and I am just about to begin," Ted said with a smile, "How was the fishing?"

Holding up the basket, Audrey said, "Would you like some bass fillets for supper?"

"Breaded, with a slice of lemon on the side," Ted said.

"I'll get these cleaned, then start on the windows," Tyler told Audrey.

Giggling, Audrey said, "Count your fingers when you finish, and remember, we want fillets." Gathering up the equipment, Audrey headed for the lodge.

Pausing a moment, Tyler asked Ted "Do you paint horses?"

"I haven't done one for quite a while," Ted said, "but I always enjoy capturing animals on canvas."

"I live with the Porter family in Eau Claire," Tyler said, "Jack Porter deals in horses. You should stop by and see them."

"I think I just may do that," Ted said. "What breeds does he have."

"Right now he has Suffolks and Friesians," said Tyler. "Friesians are the most beautiful horses I have ever seen. Expect me there within a month."

Tyler was humming to himself as he stood on the ladder washing windows at the lodge. Alma Dixon came out of the lodge carrying a large glass of lemonade.

"Please take a break and have some lemonade," she said, "you should be relaxing, not working."

Tyler stepped down from the ladder and took the glass. "Thank you," he said, taking a long drink. "How did you ever let Audrey talk you into this?" asked Alma.

Grinning, Tyler said, "Actually, I offered to do it. For me it is relaxing."

"What sort of work do you do?" Alma asked.

"I'm a deputy sheriff in Eau Claire," Tyler said. "This sure beats arresting people."

Alma laughed and said, "I'm sure it does. Well, if it makes you happy, keep going. You are doing a great job, and thanks for cleaning the fish."

When the dishes were done, Audrey grabbed two bottles of root beer from the ice cooler. "Let's go sit on the picnic table and watch the sunset," she said, handing Tyler one of the bottles. The sun was about to touch the horizon when they sat down. The lake was smooth, like a pane of shaded glass.

Taking a sip of her drink, Audrey said, "I want to know about you Tyler, just start at the beginning and stop at today."

Blowing out a slow breath, Tyler took a drink of his root beer, and began. He started with his earliest memories of the orphanage, Mother Superior Veronica, and Mary. He tried his best to explain about the war, and his role in it. It was easier to tell her about the Porters, and how they had taken him in after Mary's death. He laughed telling her about his winter logging. He described his job as a deputy, and the shooting that had brought him here. Audrey listened intently, never interrupting, only nodding her head occasionally.

"Today was the nicest day I've had in years, because I got to spend most of it with you." Taking a sip of his drink, Tyler said, "now I would like to hear your story."

As the twilight slowly descended upon them, Audrey began. "My father, whom I never knew, was a brakeman on the Soo-line Railroad. I was told by George that he died when a faulty coupling let go. My mother died giving me life six months later." A tear glistened on her cheek in the moonlight. "Alma is my mother's older sister. She and George had no children, so they took me as their own." motioning with her hand she said, "this is the only life I have ever known. I love this place. Audrey's head slowly sank to her chest as she continued. "I was engaged to a young man named Phillip, who went off to that stupid war and got killed."

Raising her head, she looked at Tyler. "I have had an

empty spot in my heart, until today." Slowly, hesitantly, Audrey reached out and took Tyler's hand. "I think you felt it at the same time I did."

Nodding his head, Tyler said, "I feel like I am dreaming, but I'm more wide awake than I have ever been." Tyler stood, took both of Audrey's hands in his and slowly pulled her to her feet. His arms went around her waist as hers encircled his neck. "I'm going to kiss you," he said softly.

"I've been waiting since this morning for this," Audrey breathed softly. It was a moment of truth for both, as they embraced.

Tyler was awake before dawn the next morning. He lay there, smiling, feeling as if the world was a wonderful place. He thought about last night with Audrey. After their first kiss, they had talked some more, then kissed some more. She had laid her face against his chest as tears dropped softly from her hazel eyes. Then they both started giggling, and could not stop! It was the happiness finding its way to the surface for both of them. Finally, they had parted, her to the lodge and him to his cabin.

Tyler got out of bed, washed, shaved and put on clean clothes, wishing he had bought more than one change. He left the cabin and strolled down to the beach. The sun was just behind the trees when the breakfast bell rang. Ted was coming from his cabin, and they entered the lodge together. Audrey was setting out flowers in vases on the tables, humming to herself.

Smiling, Ted said, "I sense a subtle change in our lovely waitress this morning. She seems quite happy."

Tyler blushed from his neck to his forehead. "Audrey and I had a long talk last night" he said, "and we will be seeing more of each other."

"That's wonderful," Ted said, "I was hoping the two of you would like each other. You both deserve all the happiness you can find."

While they were doing the morning dishes, Audrey said, "Today is laundry day. If you have anything that needs washing, bring it over."

"I will," Tyler said, "I have to go into McKinley this morning. Is there anything you need?"

Thinking a moment she said, "I want to bake some pies later, could you bring back some lard?"

"What kind of Pies?" Tyler asked.

Laughing, Audrey replied, "Apple pies, they are Ted's favorite."

"Mine too," Tyler said, "I'll be back in about an hour."

At the gas station telephone, Tyler called the sheriff's office and told Jeff he would be back to work Monday morning.

"It's only been a week," Jeff said, "are you sure you're ready?"

"Yes," Tyler said, "everything is fine. I will tell you all about it Monday." At the local market, Tyler got the lard. Just inside the door was a display of something that caught his eye. On a wooden rack were four fishing rods, each four feet long, with reels. Picking one up, he examined it, then did a short cast. With a small sinker tied on the end, the line zinged off the reel to land ten feet away. Laughing in surprise, he took the rod outside and tried it again. This time the line went over twenty feet. Reeling it in, he took the rod inside and bought two. 'Audrey is going to love this,' he thought.

Back at the lodge, Tyler showed Audrey how to cast and reel back in. "I love this!" Audrey cried. "We have to try these out this evening. Right now, there is something you can do for me."

"You name it," Tyler said.

"Boat 2, the brown one, is leaking by the transom," Audrey said. "It needs caulking and a coat of paint."

"I'll do it while the pies are baking," Tyler said.

The Doberstein brothers had left, gone back to Beloit. Audrey thoroughly cleaned the cabin, getting it ready for the older couple expected to be arriving today. As she worked, she thought about Tyler. He would be leaving soon, and she needed to know when he would return. She was in love, and it was wonderful and agonizing at the same time. Would the distance between them change how he felt? George and Alma needed her here, could Tyler accept that? And what about his family, the Porter's, how would they feel about her? She felt alive again, her heart beat faster at the sight and sound of Tyler. 'We can work it out,' Audrey thought, 'if Tyler loves me, we can work it out.'

Tyler found he liked working with the boat. He gently pushed the rope caulking in around the keel. With the twelve foot boat up on saw horses, he began brushing a new coat of paint on. 'I could do this for a living,' he thought. As he worked, he was deciding how to tell Audrey he was leaving in a few days. He would return as often as he could, for as long as it took. Could he give up being a deputy for a life here at the Lodge with Audrey? How would the Porters feel if he left? These things needed to be sorted out, and Tyler would do it. He loved Audrey, there was no question about that. His life now felt complete, the missing piece to the puzzle that was his life had been found.

CHAPTER TWENTY-TWO

The boat sat motionless in the water as Tyler and Audrey sat facing each other. The supper dishes were done and the new couple had arrived and were settled in their cabin. "I have to leave tomorrow," Tyler said, "but I will be back in two weeks. Ellis and I take turns working the weekends."

"I know you have to go," Audrey said, "but I'll miss you terribly. I can't imagine us apart."

Taking her hands in his, he spoke firmly. "The first thing I am going to do when I get back to Eau Claire is buy a car. Then I am going to bring you home to meet the Porters."

"Do you think they will like me?" Audrey asked softly.

Smiling, Tyler said, "Jack, Andy, Tom and especially Julia are going to love you."

"George and Alma can do without me for one weekend" Audrey said, "but I need to be here for them."

Squeezing her hands tenderly, Tyler replied "things will work out, we just need to make plans as we go. I can't quit being a deputy right now. It will take Jeff time to find someone new and get them trained."

"I told George and Alma that we were in love," Audrey said, "they are both happy for us, but they are wondering about their future."

Smiling, Tyler leaned over and kissed her. "Their future, and ours, is going to be wonderful," he said.

Tyler drove into the Porter's yard about four o'clock. Jack and Tom were working with a team of Percherons. Julia came out the front door wiping her hands on her apron.

Tyler sat on the cycle a moment, smiling. "I'll bet you were baking bread," he said.

"For your information Mr. Smarty, I was making biscuits," Julia said laughing.

Jack walked over and asked, "How was the cycle ride?"

"It was fun," Tyler said, "But tomorrow I am buying a car."

Tom had joined them, and asked, "You can use the truck whenever you want, why do you need a car?"

"Because the cycle only holds one," Tyler said grinning.

Julia took hold of Tyler's forearm and looked into his eyes. A smile spread across her face as she said, "You have met someone, haven't you Tyler?"

Blushing and grinning, he said, "Her name is Audrey. She lives with her aunt and uncle at Sugar Lake Lodge." Jack and Tom stood with their mouths open staring at Tyler.

Turning to Tom, Julia said, "Go get Andy. Tyler is going to tell us all about his new friend."

Julia poured iced tea as they sat around the kitchen table.

"How was the fishing?" Jack asked.

"We can talk about the fishing later," Julia said, "I want to hear about Audrey."

Tyler told them all about Audrey.

"Can she cook?" Andy asked.

"She makes a great apple pie," Tyler said.

"Does she bait her own hook?" Jack asked.

"Grubs, worms or minnows," Tyler said, "and I bought her one of those new casting rods. No fish in Sugar Lake is safe."

"When can we meet her?" Tom wanted to know.

"This coming weekend I have duty," Tyler said, "and if it is alright with you folks, I would like to bring her here to meet you all the weekend after."

Julia was standing behind Tyler. She laid her hands on his shoulders and said, "She will be welcome as one of the family."

On Monday morning, Tyler drove the motorcycle behind the office, parked it and covered it with the tarp. Ellis drove in, parked and got out of his patrol car. "I'm glad your back," he said, "but I thought you were taking two weeks off."

"Only needed one," Tyler said, "and I've got some news for you and Jeff."

As they walked into the office, Jeff was behind his desk. "Glad you're back" he said, "feeling better?"

"Better than I have felt in years," Tyler told him.

"That must have been some vacation," Ellis said with a grin.

"It was. I met the girl I intend to marry."

For a moment, the only sound in the office was the ticking of the wall clock.

"Run that by me again," Jeff said, "did I hear you say marriage?"

"I haven't asked her yet," Tyler said, "but I think she will say yes."

Laughing, Ellis grabbed Tyler's hand and shook it. "You really know how to take a vacation. Where did you meet her?"

It took a half hour for Tyler to tell them about Audrey. He answered all their questions, then asked, "Can I take an hour off? I need to buy a car."

Ellis snapped his fingers and pointed at Tyler. "Doc Bristol just traded in his Packard for a new Cadillac. It's a 1918, and Doc never took it out of state."

"Is it over at Hale's car lot?" Tyler asked.

"It's not even on the lot yet," Ellis said, "it's in the garage getting an oil change and new tires."

"Ellis. Take Tyler will take you over there" Jeff said, "then get right back here, we have some planning to do."

Howard Hale slapped the fender of the Packard saying "This beauty goes for $400 and not a penny less."

Scratching behind his ear, Ellis asked him "how much money would you have lost if we had not caught those bank robbers?" Without batting an eye, Howard replied "$350, and not a penny less."

"I'll take it," Tyler said. "I'll pick it up and pay you after my shift is done."

"We have a cattle thief in the county," Jeff said when the two returned. "Hiram Juergens raises Herefords. Last

Monday, he reported one heifer missing, This morning he says another is missing."

"Stealing one at a time doesn't make any sense," Ellis said.

"Unless you can only haul one at a time," Tyler said.

"Must be somebody local," Jeff said, "probably working alone."

"But where would he keep them?" Ellis said with a frown.

Smiling, Tyler said, "He isn't keeping them, he is selling them."

"Nobody around here would buy one," Jeff said, "Hiram is the only man around raising Hereford's, so anyone would know they were stolen."

"Hampton," Tyler said.

"What about Hampton?" Jeff asked.

"Every Wednesday morning Hampton, Minnesota has a livestock sale," Tyler said, "I've gone there with Jack, looking for horses."

"That means whoever is doing the stealing is crossing the river, probably at Prescott," Ellis said.

"I want both of you to be at the Prescott bridge Wednesday morning," Jeff said, "stop anyone towing a trailer. We just might get lucky."

Doyle Chalmers was not happy, in fact, he was cursing the world and his role in it. Doyle was 5 foot 10 inches tall, and going to fat. He was almost bald, except for the fringe of brown hair around his growing bald spot. At 47 years old, Doyle was again, unemployed. He had worked at the brewery for years, until it closed. Then he got fired from the sawmill after he showed up drunk for the second time. He was renting the house on the old Ziwicke farm, six miles south of Eau Claire. The barn on the property was a wreck, but still standing. Parked in the barn was an old one stall horse trailer with one flat tire. There was a trailer hitch on his 1915 Ford, and Doyle's brain went into overdrive. He knew about the livestock sales in Hampton and decided to become a cattle rustler.

'Juergens won't miss a few head of beef,' he thought, 'he must have over a hundred cows.' As usual, Doyle was wrong.

After patching the tire, Doyle had stolen the first heifer on a Sunday night. He got $50 for it at Hampton the following Wednesday morning. By the time he got home, the other tire on the trailer was flat. He fixed it, and now had another heifer ready to go. 'At least I can pay the rent and eat for a while,' he thought, 'sure glad I don't have a wife and kids to look after.'

At five o'clock Wednesday morning, Ellis and Tyler were at the Prescott bridge. The sun was nowhere to be seen yet, but dark was giving way to a gray light. An occasional car passed them, none with a trailer. By six am, a yellow and violet pastel light inched it's way over the horizon. There was more traffic now, but still no cars with trailers. At 6:15 a truck hauling a double trailer was stopped. The driver let them look inside. Two horses stood eating hay. "Going to Hampton," the driver told them. Tyler waved him on.

As Doyle neared the bridge, traffic seemed to be moving way to slow. 'Must have been an accident,' thought Doyle.

Then he saw the deputies. There was no place to turn off or turn around, he had to keep going. At the bridge, one deputy stepped in front of the Ford while the other stepped up to his door.

"We need to look in your trailer," Ellis told him. In a moment of panic, Doyle stomped on the gas pedal. The Ford jerked forward, coughed, and stalled out. Tyler had jumped aside, then swung onto the running board on the passenger side.

"Hands in the air!" Ellis yelled, drawing his Colt. Doyle looked to his right, and saw Tyler pointing another pistol at him.

Ellis yanked open the driver's door and pulled Doyle out by his shirt. "Hands behind your back," he ordered.

Doyle kept hollering, "Don't shoot me! Don't shoot me!" Doyle was placed in the back of the patrol car.

Tyler said, "I'll go across, turn around and follow you back to town."

Every afternoon she could get free, Audrey took the boat out and practiced casting with her new rod. After the second backlash, she used her thumb to control the line after the bait hit the water. It was like a kind of therapy for her, with Tyler gone. He had called her twice, and just hearing his voice thrilled her.

Every morning, Ted asked about Tyler. "When I finish this painting, I am going to the Porter farm to do a painting of horses," he said.

"Tyler will be here next Friday afternoon," Audrey said, "and we are going to visit the Porter's."

Smiling, Ted said, "That's wonderful! I am sure you will enjoy it. Has he asked you to marry him?"

Blushing and smiling, Audrey said, "We have not talked about marriage yet, we just met, and are getting to know each other."

With a sad smile, Ted said, "I plan on painting a wedding picture for you, with Tyler as the lucky groom."

Julia had Andy and Tom washing windows and beating rugs. "What is she doing now?" Andy asked as he wiped his brow. "

"I hear the sewing machine going," Tom said, "I think she is sewing new curtains."

"Do you think Tyler will marry this girl and move away?" Andy asked.

"It's too soon to tell" Tom answered, "but if he is bringing this girl to meet us, it's possible."

"It won't be the same without him," Andy said.

"Well, he isn't gone yet," Tom said, "so just keep beating the dust out of that rug."

CHAPTER TWENTY-THREE

The Packard ran so quiet that Tyler could hardly hear it from inside. He was smiling as he drove, thinking about Audrey. Her smile, her laugh and her excitement at catching big fish. 'I am in love,' he thought, 'and I am pretty sure she loves me.' He turned onto Milkweed road, and in no time the lodge came in sight.

Audrey and Alma were on the porch as he drove up. Audrey wore a yellow sundress with tiny pink flowers. It was the first time Tyler had seen her in anything but jeans and a shirt. As Tyler stepped out of the car, Audrey skipped down the steps and clapped her hands, laughing.

"It's beautiful!" she cried as she threw her arms around his neck and kissed him."

My, what a fine looking auto," Alma said.

Coming up for air, Tyler said, "it belonged to the local Doctor. It's almost new."

George walked out of the lodge, smiling. In his hand was a small suitcase. He handed it to Tyler saying, "Audrey has been like a kid at Christmas waiting for you."

"I will have her back on Sunday afternoon," Tyler said. Opening the passenger door, Audrey slid in on the smooth leather seat.

"This is wonderful," she said with a sigh. They waved goodbye to George and Alma as they drove away.

"Next week, Ellis and Claudia are getting married," Tyler told her, "I will be his best man."

"Will someone be taking pictures," Audrey asked.

"The photo studio in Eau Claire will be there," Tyler said, "so there will be photographs."

"Wonderful!" Audrey said, "I want to see you all dressed up in a suit and tie."

"I guess there is a first time for everything," Tyler said laughing. Soon Tyler turned off the highway and drove slowly into the Porter's yard. Jack, Tom, Julia, Andy and Molly had been waiting on the porch, and all walked down to the Packard.

Molly jumped up to get her head scratched as Tyler moved around the car and opened the passenger door. Audrey stepped out, smiling and slightly blushing. Holding her hand. Tyler said, "Everyone, this is Audrey Dixon."

Jack was the first to come forward. Taking Audrey's hand he said, "I am Jackson Porter and it is a pleasure to meet you."

Tom was next, and said, "you are as pretty as Tyler said."

Andy blushed so hard, it looked like a sunburn. He shook her hand and smiled. Without waiting, Audrey took both Julia's hands and said, "Your Julia. Tyler talks about you all the time."

Now Julia was blushing. "All good things, I hope" she said with a smile.

"All wonderful things," Audrey said. Molly trotted over, sat down right in front of Audrey and held out her paw. Giggling, Audrey knelt and shook the paw, then scratched her head. "Hello Molly Tyler talks about you too."

"I have some cold iced tea in the parlor," Julia said, "let's go in and get to know each other."

The day passed too quickly. Julia and Audrey bonded like a mother and daughter. Audrey delighted in talking gardening and cooking. Jack showed off his Friesian horses.

"Oh my lord, they are so beautiful!" Audrey exclaimed.

"Ted will be here soon to do a painting of them."

Andy had cleaned up the forge just to impress Audrey, which it did. Tom trotted out the Suffolks and took them through their paces. The dinner bell rang and all went to the backyard where the picnic table was laid out with chicken, corn on the cob, sliced tomatoes and cucumbers, salad and homemade bread. "I wish I had time to do more baking," Audrey said, "I know Tyler likes apple pie."

"That's what we are having for dessert," Tom said, laughing. As the sun began it's slow descent, it was time to leave.

Audrey hugged everyone, including Molly. "You must visit the lodge and meet George and Alma," she told them.

"Has the fishing been good?" Jack asked.

"With my new casting rod, it has improved," Audrey said laughing. They waved as the Packard rolled down the drive.

"Next time you visit, we will drive to Madison," Tyler said, "I want you to meet Mother Superior Veronica. I wrote and told her about you and she would like to meet you."

"You talk so much about her," Audrey said, "she must be a remarkable woman."

"She loves children," Tyler said, "many orphans have been saved because of her." As the excitement of the day began to fade, Audrey sighed and laid her head on Tyler's shoulder as he drove.

"It was a wonderful weekend," she said softly, "I am sad it has to end."

"I will be sad when I get you home," Tyler said, "it will be a week before I see you again."

"I will miss you every day," Audrey sighed, "so you must call during the week."

Tyler said as he kissed the top of her head. "I will."

"I finally got the go-ahead from city hall to hire two more deputies," Jeff told Tyler and Ellis on Monday morning.

"The bank robbery must have scared them more than we thought," Ellis said.

"Do you have anyone in mind?" Tyler asked.

"Not at the moment," Jeff said, "but if you know anybody who might be a good prospect, let me know."

"All I can think about right now is my wedding this weekend," Ellis said.

"Getting a little nervous?" Jeff asked.

Blushing, Ellis said, "Sometimes I wonder if I'm doing the right thing."

Tyler patted his shoulder. "If you love her, it's the right thing."

It was late in the afternoon when Tyler noticed the smoke on the horizon. There was no wind, and the dark gray smoke was rising straight up. Turning off the county road, Tyler found himself on a gravel road that seemed familiar. 'This is the road to the Koznicky farm,' he thought, and he was right.

The old house was ablaze as he drove in the yard. There was no one around, no cars parked there, nobody in sight. In the distance, he heard the hand-cranked siren of the volunteer fire truck. It pulled into the drive as close as safety permitted and several men jumped off.

"Hold it guys, just hold it!" yelled Bernie Albright, the fire chief. The roof of the house slowly caved in, sending sparks and embers flying up. Bernie walked along the front and side of the burning house, as close as he could get. Walking back, he said, "It would be a waste of water right now, let it burn, then put out the ashes."

Walking over to Tyler, he asked, "Do you know how it started?"

"I just got here myself," Tyler said, "and I didn't see anyone leaving."

Bernie took off his helmet and wiped his thinning hair with a handkerchief. "It's been vacant since that woman got killed here" he said. "Probably a good thing it's gone now."

"I'll write up a report when I get back to town," Tyler said. The sides and front slowly fell into the fire, sending up more sparks. 'Yes,' thought Tyler, 'probably a good thing.'

CHAPTER TWENTY-FOUR

The Mathewson brothers, from Nickerson, Minnesota were as opposite as two brothers could be. Leland, 'Lee', was 31 years old, Tall, lean, full head of brown hair and divorced, with no children. Hoyt was 35, short, stout, thinning blonde hair, single and smoked cigars. They had tried farming, but neither liked the hours or the work. Hoyt bought a well-used Studebaker two ton truck, and they went into the hauling business. It proved more to their liking, and soon Lee had his own two ton Chevrolet truck.

When the Volstead act went into effect, some well-dressed men from Chicago came calling. Hoyt and lee began hauling truckloads of barreled whiskey from Canada, and the money was rolling in. They would load up at Thunder Bay, Canada and deliver to Chicago, Illinois whenever Hoyt got the call. A cousin, Delbert Mathewson, was recruited to haul with his Ford truck.

However, problems arose when rival gangs began hijacking each other's trucks. The Mathewson's began hiring armed men to ride 'shotgun' on their trucks. Soon, the word was out – if you wanted a Mathewson truck, it would cost you. Most hijackers backed off, a few did not.

The Mathewson trucks left Thunder bay at dusk. The weather was clear, with a full moon. The miles rolled by and soon they crossed into Minnesota. At Willow River they stopped for gas and a hot coffee. They crossed into Wisconsin at Taylor Falls, and headed south along the river road, turning east at River Falls. The hijackers struck ten miles out of Martell. A roadblock with two cars and men armed with shotguns. Hoyt was driving the lead truck. He laid on the horn, and stepped on the gas.

SLAM! BANG!

The big Studebaker truck hit the cars head on! One slid sideways into the ditch, the other rolled over on its side, steam hissing from its radiator. The three trucks rolled on into the dawn. A black Cadillac roared out of a side road and began shooting at the trucks. Delbert, in the last truck, had a front tire shot out and went off the road. The shotgun rider in Lee's truck returned fire, but was hit when a Thompson sub-machine gun began its rapid fire. Lee was also hit, and rolled to a stop as he blacked out.

Hoyt and his shotgun rider swerved, trying to knock the Cadillac into the ditch. Then a shotgun blast took out Hoyt's rider and slammed a load of buckshot into Hoyt's right side. Hoyt swerved again, this time knocking the Cadillac into a steep ditch. Knowing he was dying, Hoyt kept driving until he slowly collapsed over the steering wheel east of Elmwood, half on and half off the road.

A farmer called the sheriff's office, yelling about a big truck blocking traffic. Jeff sent both Ellis and Tyler to check it out.

"I'll bet it's those whiskey haulers," Ellis said, "probably drunk." Several farmers were waiting for them at the truck, one of them on a Farmall tractor. Ellis walked over to the truck and pounded on the door.

"Wake up in there," he yelled.

Tyler was looking at the door of the truck and saw something slowly dripping from the bottom of the door. Looking closer, he tapped Ellis on the shoulder. "Blood."

Ellis stepped up on the running board and looked in the window. After a minute, he stepped down, his face pale. "Looks like the driver and passenger are both dead."

Tyler nodded. "Is the shift lever in neutral?"

Looking in again, Ellis said, "Yeah, it looks to be in neutral. I'll have the farmer with the tractor tow the truck into town. You and I better backtrack and see what else we can find." About five miles further back, they found Leland's body laying head down in the ditch, dead. The passenger's body lay a few yards away, clutching a shotgun in his lifeless hand. The truck was gone.

"Looks like a hijacking gone wrong," Tyler said, "I'll leave a marker and have the ambulance pick them up." Tying his red handkerchief onto a stout stick, he jammed it into the dirt next to the body.

At the outskirts of Eau Claire they passed the tractor hauling the truck. At the office, Jeff was waiting to find out what happened. He listened as Tyler and Ellis told him what they found. "I'll call the FBI and have them come and get the truck and the bodies," he said. Maybe they know who the dead men are."

"The truck has Minnesota plates," Tyler said, "probably hauling whiskey down from Canada."

The cloudy skies and brisk wind on Saturday did not interfere with Ellis and Claudia's wedding. Claudia's father, Calvin, looked uncomfortable in his new suit bought just for this occasion. As he walked Claudia down the aisle, her mother sniffled and dabbed at her eyes with a dainty white lace handkerchief. Ellis was slightly pale, but his eyes had a determined look. Joining hands at the altar, the young couple repeated their vows, traded rings, and kissed. The photographer had the wedding party wait as the guests were ushered from the church.

Then, after several pictures were taken, then all left for the Elks Lodge where the reception was held. No alcohol was served, but plenty of great food for the hungry crowd. A polka band took the stage and almost everyone, old and young, were out on the dance floor. Several times men would slip out the back door and re-enter later, smiling, wiping their mouths and smelling faintly of brandy. Tyler and Ellis were not among them.

Theodore Boehm arrived at the Porter farm on Sunday afternoon. Jack and Tom had gone fishing, Tyler was helping Ellis and Claudia move, Andy was napping in the hammock and Julia was on the front porch knitting a half-finished wool sock. Molly raised her head at the sound of the auto, then got up and ambled down the steps.

Ted got out of his car and walked to the house. "Good afternoon," he said, smiling. "You must be Julia. I'm Ted Boehm. Tyler invited me to stop by."

Julia laid down her knitting and stood. "Please come in the kitchen for some iced tea," she said smiling. Entering the kitchen, the aroma of strawberry and rhubarb pie tickled Ted's nose.

Seated at the kitchen table, Ted said, "Tyler and I became quite good friends when he visited Sugar Lake Lodge."

"He is a wonderful young man who has been dealt harshly by life," Julia said, "but since he met Audrey, his outlook has greatly improved."

"They do make a loving couple," Ted agreed, "I take great pride in having introduced them to each other."

Julia took Ted down to the corral where a Friesian mare was drinking at the water trough. "God must have been in a very artistic mood when he created such a beautiful animal," Ted said softly. The mare lifted her head, saw Julia at the railing and walked over. Julia reached out her hand and the horse lowered its head to be petted.

"I can start my drawing tomorrow morning," Ted said, "can you tell me of a good hotel in town where I might stay?"

"You will stay here," Julia said firmly, "it will save you the drive back and forth every day, plus you get fresh pie after supper."

Laughing, Ted said, "it is a wonderful offer and I will accept on one condition. I will set the room rate and pay you accordingly at the completion of my work."

Holding out her hand, Julia said, "That is a deal I will shake on."

"Then I will take my things into the house," Ted said, "and we can talk more about the future of Tyler and Audrey."

Ted met the Porter family at supper that night. The fishing had been good at Beech Lake – the perch and bluegill had been feeding. Jack had tried out Tyler's casting rod, and was impressed. Tyler joined in cleaning while Julia set about frying the catch. A garden salad and oven baked potatoes were laid out on the picnic table. Jack gave Ted the history of the Friesian horse.

"It is difficult to imagine an animal that beautiful used for such an ugly purpose," Ted remarked.

"Thankfully, the breed survived," Jack said, "and I have had several serious inquiries about buying the offspring."

"I look forward to starting sketching tomorrow," Ted said as he buttered a steaming potato.

Jeff Patten had some news on Monday morning. "I heard back from the FBI," he said, "they identified two of the men that were killed as Hoyt and Leland Mathewson, brothers, from Minnesota. The other two they are still trying to identify. The truck was loaded with barrels of whiskey."

"What happens now?" Ellis asked.

"The feds want a detailed report," Jeff said, "so you and Tyler sit down, write it out and I'll send it to Madison."

CHAPTER TWENTY-FIVE

Sugar Lake Lodge was booked solid. All three cabins and two rooms in the lodge held guests from all over the state. Two older couples from Green Bay had rooms in the lodge. A party of three men from Oshkosh shared cabin 3, a couple with a young boy were in no. 2, and two newlyweds had cabin no. 1. Alma, George, and Audrey were busy from dawn to dusk keeping everyone happy.

The boats were on the water constantly, and the bait was running low. When Tyler showed up Friday afternoon, he saw the problem and offered to help. "Our bait guy just delivered the minnows and worms," Audrey said as she wiped her brow with a bandanna, "I just wish we had one more boat."

Smiling, Tyler kissed her forehead. "I'll be back in an hour." True to his word, he returned with a twelve foot boat tied on top of the Packard and a pair of oars sticking out the side window.

"Where did you get it?" Audrey cried.

"On the way up here, I saw a yard sign that had a boat for sale," Tyler said, "so I went back and bought it for $25."

Audrey started laughing. "I dream of a knight in shining armor, riding a white horse, and God sends me a deputy in a Packard!"

"I'll back the car down to the beach and my princess in a flannel shirt and jeans can help me unload it."

"I know we were supposed to go to Madison this weekend to meet Mother Veronica," Audrey said, "but I can't leave George and Alma to handle this crowd alone."

"I will call and tell her the problem," Tyler said squeezing her shoulder, "She will understand. Now, what else do you need help with?"

"I've got a sink full of dishes that need washing, linens to change and potatoes that need peeling" Audrey said, "you start in the kitchen and I will do the cabins."

"A hug and a kiss will get me started," Tyler said smiling. The hug was long as they gathered strength from each other. The kiss was longer, a sharing of joy and peace.

By nine o'clock that night, the dishes were done and all was quiet. Tyler sat on the picnic table watching the full moon cast a shadowy light over the lake. Audrey came out of the kitchen, sat next to him and offered the bottle she was carrying.

Taking a sip, Tyler smiled. "Good beer," he said.

"The guys from Oshkosh gave us a six-pack," she said, "I think we earned it today." Tyler put an arm around her shoulder and pulled her close. For a time, they just sat and sipped the beer until it was gone. It was the being together that was important, the caring and sharing. Then Tyler moved his arm from her shoulder and took both her hands in his.

Looking into her hazel eyes, he said, "I like it here at the lake. I could live here, on one condition."

"What is that?" Audrey asked.

"Will you marry me" Tyler asked.

Tears glistened at the corner of Audrey's eyes. "Yes Tyler Braun, I will marry you," she said softly, and sealed the words with a kiss.

By Sunday afternoon, things had quieted down at the lodge, the two older couples had left in the morning and the men from Oshkosh would be leaving by evening. Tyler and Audrey sat George and Alma down and told them of Tyler's proposal. George beamed like a proud father while Audrey and Alma hugged and cried.

"We don't know yet when the wedding will be," Tyler said, "I have to give Jeff time to hire a replacement deputy. I want to live here at the lake and help run the lodge."

"It is like an answer to a prayer," Alma said, "George and I were worried about being able to take care of the lodge as we get older."

"Not to mention, we now have another boat to care for," Audrey said laughing, "and I promise there will always be a sink full of dishes."

"I asked Audrey to marry me, and she said yes" Tyler told the Porter family over Sunday night supper.

Julia's eyes were misty as she hugged Tyler. "I am so happy for you," she said, "she is a wonderful girl."

Jack, Tom, Andy and Ted all shook his hand and slapped his back. "When is the wedding?" Jack asked.

"I intend to live at Sugar Lake Lodge," Tyler said, "so

I have to give Jeff time to hire a new deputy. Then we will decide on a wedding day."

"Congratulations" Ellis and Jeff said after hearing Tyler's news.

Jeff asked "Will this change your deputy status?"

"It will," Tyler answered, "I will be moving to the lodge, so you will need to hire someone else."

"I have two new guys in training now," Jeff said, "

"I will start looking for your replacement this week, but you will be hard to replace."

"I sure hate to lose you," Ellis said, "we worked so well as a team."

Nodding his head, Tyler said, "We make a great team, and I will always be thankful for that."

That afternoon, the peaceful September day came to a violent end. The gray clouds moved in, pushed by a wind from the northwest. The funnel slammed into the ground at Clayton, churning and pushing, blowing apart everything in its path. A railroad depot disappeared into the howling tornado, followed by the church. Broken boards and shingles were spit out the sides like unwanted chaff. Newly set telephone poles were torn from the earth and tossed aside. Electric power lines, freed from their poles waved about, seeming like angry black snakes, searching for prey. Barns, silos, houses and machinery fed the churning wind.

The town of Prairie Farm was almost entirely destroyed as the tornado descended upon it with a fury. Homes, businesses, two churches and the school were reduced to piles of broken wood and shattered glass. Roaring south east, the screaming beast of wind let loose of the ground and passed over the small village of Jim Falls, punching back into the ground a half-mile further on. One hundred year old trees were ripped from the earth and cast aside like an unwanted child's toy. Everything in its path was chewed up and spit out.

The people of Stanley ran for whatever cover they could find. Automobiles were thrown into trees, the courthouse roof was blown off, logs from the sawmill were thrown about like blunt spears, crashing through the stained glass windows of the Lutheran church. Then, like a giant locomotive running out of steam, the funnel retreated back into the sky on the outskirts of Thorp. The quiet afterward was eerie.

The call went out for help. Jeff sent Tyler and Ellis. With a truck donated by the Valley Sawmill Company, and loaded with blankets, canned goods, tents, clothing and first-aid supplies, the two men drove to Jim Falls where a command center had been set up. They parked next to the one room school house being used by the National Guard as an operations room. Telephones had been installed to keep Madison informed of daily operations.

A Major Lavoy was in charge, and shook their hands. "I'll have my men unload your truck. I need you men directing traffic. People are stopping to take pictures of the damage, and they blocking the roads so the ambulances can't get through." Pointing outside he said, "Take that Army car to Stanley and tell Captain Van Epps I sent you."

Red Cross doctors and nurses treated the wounded lined up outside their tent. Ambulances carrying as many as they could, took those with serious injuries and broken bones to the Eau Claire hospital. By five o'clock, only one death had been reported. Volunteers were put to work making sandwiches and coffee for the workers and the wounded. Farm animals were rounded up and given a fenced off pasture with a water tank, filled by a pumper truck. The horses, cows and mules were safe until their owners showed up to claim them. An emergency generator arrived from Eau Claire – a huge gasoline powered machine that would give light into the night.

By Wednesday, Tyler and Ellis were in their empty truck and driving home. "I haven't seen that much damage done since the shelling during the war," Ellis said.

"It will take months to clean everything up," Tyler said, "this morning I saw six men hauling those logs out of the church."

"All those telephone and electric lines will need to be strung up again," Ellis said shaking his head.

"I'm glad Eau Claire was spared," Tyler said, "imagine the damage that would have happened."

The Porter family and Ted were glad to see Tyler drive in that afternoon. "You have to call Audrey as soon as you can," Julia said, "she is frantic with worry."

"I will," Tyler said. Turning to Ted he asked, "How is the painting coming?"

"It's almost half finished," Ted said, "this is going to be the finest painting I have done in years."

"He won't let us see it until it's done," Tom said, "but the drawing he gave to Julia is the best I have ever seen."

"I'm going to have it framed to hang in the house," Julia said with a smile.

Tyler walked in the house and called Audrey. "I was so worried about you," she said, "I've been driving poor Julia crazy."

"Ellis and I are both fine," Tyler said. "The national Guard is in charge of the cleanup, so I am back on duty."

"Can you get away this weekend," Audrey asked.

"Yes I have the weekend off," Tyler said, "this time we will go to see Mother Veronica."

"I can't wait to meet her," Audrey told him.

"We are taking the train from Cumberland to Madison," Tyler told Audrey on Friday evening.

"I thought we would drive," Audrey said.

"On the way here it took over an hour longer than usual," Tyler told her, "the roads are blocked with trucks and construction equipment working on the tornado damage. We will actually save time taking the train."

"What time do we leave?" Audrey asked.

"The train leaves Cumberland at 6am, and gets into Madison at noon," Tyler said.

Smiling, Audrey said, "I haven't been on a train in years. It will be fun."

Mother Superior Veronica was waiting when Tyler and Audrey arrived by taxi. Stepping forward with hands outstretched and smiling, she greeted them. "Tyler, your eyes tell me you have found the happiness you were seeking."

Blushing, Tyler said, "Mother Veronica, meet Audrey Dixon." Clasping hands, the two women shared a moment of silent joy.

"The sisters have prepared a lunch for us," Veronica said, "and two children are waiting to greet you." As they entered the dining hall, a girl and boy stood there waiting. "Tyler, do you recall Ruthann and Tim Koznicky?"

The girl and boy looked nothing like the two children Tyler had delivered to the orphanage month before. Both were happy, smiling youths. "I remember these two very well," Tyler said, " but they sure look different now."

"Tim is becoming one of our young baseball players," said Mother Veronica, "and Ruthann is mastering our mathematics class."

Kneeling, Tyler asked them, "are you happy?"

"You promised we would be," Ruthann said, "and we are." Tim grinned and nodded his head. The two ran off to join friends and Veronica, Audrey and Tyler sat to have lunch and talk of the months past and what lay ahead.

"We will be married soon in Eau Claire," Tyler said, "you must be there."

"You have my solemn promise to attend," Mother Veronica said, "it will bring me great joy."

The steady rolling motion of the train soon put Audrey to sleep on the way home. Tyler was awake, thinking back on his life. The war had taken him into manhood and given him the self-reliance to survive. He lived within himself, keeping any close attachments at bay, until he met Audrey. Looking down at her now, his heart swelled with the thought of spending his life with her. With his arm around her shoulders, he gently pulled her closer to him. In her sleep, she smiled.

CHAPTER TWENTY-SIX

Two new deputies were waiting in Jeff's office when Tyler and Ellis arrived Monday morning. Bradley Parsons was 21 years old, six foot tall, brown hair and eyes and lean. Nelson Frye was 23 years old, 5 foot ten inches, dark hair, blue eyes, and stocky. Bradley had been in the Army Quartermaster Corps. He had not left the states during the war. Nelson had joined the Coast Guard three years before the war began, and was a training NCO during the war. Neither was married.

"I want them to ride along with you two for the first week," Jeff said, "introduce them to people and get them comfortable with the routine."

Ellis looked the new men over and said, "Nelson, you ride with me." Pinning on their new badges, the deputies left the room.

Tyler and Bradley Parsons drove west out of Eau Claire, taking a county road with light traffic. "The whiskey haulers like to stay off the main roads" Tyler explained, "they will detour around large cities whenever possible."

"How do you know when you see one?" Bradley asked.

"Any truck covered with a tarp is usually hauling whiskey,"

Tyler said, "also look for Minnesota or Illinois license plates." Turning south on another county road, they saw a roadside diner and gas station. Parked off to the side were two large Chevrolet trucks with their loads covered in canvas tarps. Both had Minnesota plates.

Smiling, Tyler said, "Let's go ask the drivers what they are hauling." Entering the diner they saw the cook talking to two men at the counter, both drinking coffee. Walking up to the counter, Tyler thumbed back his hat, smiled, and said, "good morning fellas, I'm deputy Braun. What are you hauling today?" Both men were in their late thirties, one going to fat with a three-day beard, the other was about average with a scar across his right cheek.

The fat one looked up from his coffee, smirked, and said, "get lost kid."

With his hand on the butt of his pistol, Tyler told the cook "Call the Sheriff's office, tell him I've got two whiskey haulers coming in." The man with the scar reached inside his jacket. Tyler's .45 came out in a flash, aimed at the man's face. Bradley also had his pistol out, poking the fat man in the back.

"Reach up and grab some air," he told the man. Slowly, the man raised his arms. Bradley patted him down, finding a .38 caliber revolver. "You too, scar face" Bradley told the other man. From a shoulder holster Bradley eased out a .45 Colt 1911 semi-auto from under the man's jacket.

The cook came back from the kitchen and told Tyler, "The sheriff is on his way."

"Hands behind your back," Tyler told the fat man. Bradley cuffed the other man. "Let's have a coffee while we wait," Tyler told the cook.

Before the coffee had cooled, Sheriff Jeff drove up in front of the diner, got out of his car and looked over the two trucks. As he walked into the diner, he said, "two more truckloads of whiskey that will never get to Chicago. Nice work guys." Bradley's grin stretched from ear to ear. Tyler smiled and sipped his coffee.

Setting down his brush, Ted sighed, "It's done." Julia had been watching and her eyes were shining with tears.

"It's beautiful" she said softly, "You are truly an artist, Ted." They were in the front parlor where the morning sun was streaming through the windows.

"It needs time to set" Ted said, "but I am convinced it may be my best painting yet."

Tom and Jack will be knocked over when they see it," Julia said.

Cleaning his brushes, Ted asked "Any word yet when Tyler and Audrey plan to marry?"

"Jeff's two new deputies started work this morning" Julia said, "so I expect to know very soon when the wedding date has been set."

Smiling, Ted said, "Usually by this time, I am on my way to New Hampshire, but I am not budging until those two are married."

Julia laughed. "You are a wonderful guest. Stay as long as you like."

At Sugar Lake Lodge, Alma and Audrey were in the kitchen. Alma was making a beef stew for dinner while Audrey rolled out dough for biscuits. They were also trying to decide on a Saturday for the wedding.

"Julia is having the wedding at the Porter house," Audrey

said, "since the lodge closes for the summer on the second weekend in October, the third Saturday in October would be the best day get married."

Alma nodded in agreement, saying, "George and I are looking forward to meeting the Porters. Tyler talks about them so much."

"They are the family he never had as a boy," Audrey said, "and he filled the empty spot in their life when Louis died."

Pausing for a moment, Alma looked at Audrey and said, "Now Tyler will fill the place in your heart that needs tender love and care."

With misty eyes, Audrey hugged Alma and kissed her cheek. "Soon he will be here with me every day, by my side, always."

After a telephone call from Tyler, Audrey called Mother Veronica. "Tyler and I have decided on the third Saturday in October for the wedding. Can you be there?" she asked.

"I will take the train from Madison, if someone will meet me at the station in Eau Claire," said Mother Veronica.

"Tyler and I will be so happy to see you again," Audrey said, "and the Porter family wants so much to meet you."

"And I wish to meet them," Mother Veronica said, "it will be a very special day for all of us."

"Ellis and I have booked the Elks Lodge for your reception," Jeff told Tyler on Monday morning. "We know the wedding is at the Porter house, but you will need more room for the guests" Ellis said.

"Thank you both," Tyler said, "I will let Julia know so she can help decorate the hall."

"Claudia saved a lot of those paper bells from our wedding," Ellis said, "I'll tell her to bring them over."

"Reverend Powers is doing the ceremony," Tyler said, "Tom has agreed to be my best man and Audrey asked Julia to be her Maid of Honor."

"Has that artist guy finished his painting?" Jeff asked.

"Ted took the train to Milwaukee yesterday with several paintings," Tyler answered, "he will be back this week for the wedding."

"Now that that is settled," Jeff said, "let's get those new deputies out on patrol."

George, Alma, and Audrey were in McKinley buying a wedding dress. Berniece Alcott was a friend of Alma's who took in sewing and did alterations. She agreed to make a dress for Audrey.

"I want just a simple white dress," Audrey stated, "no long train or fancy lace."

Smiling, Berniece said, "I have several pictures I can show you." George waited patiently in a rocker on the front porch while the women chose just the right dress. It took an hour, including the measurements, to finalize the agreement. "I will have it ready in three days," Berniece promised.

Julia and Tom were shopping for a dress for Julia and a new suit for Tom. "You also need a haircut," Julia said, "and we still have to get Andy in a suit. I don't think he has ever owned one."

Chuckling, Tom said, "the only one who could get Andy to wear a suit is Tyler, and I don't think he will ask him to."

"Well, at least I will buy him a tie to wear," Julie sighed. "It's wonderful and painful at the same time. I am so happy he found someone, but now he will be leaving us."

Putting his arm around his wife, Tom said, "We can visit them whenever we want. I am looking forward to seeing the lake and the lodge."

Jack was deep in thought, remembering that first day Tyler had walked into his life. A cold, hungry and lonely young man looking for a friend. Tyler had cried when he was told that Louis had died. He did not replace Louis in Jack's heart, but he did make the loss easier to bear, and for that Jack was grateful. Now Jack wanted to do something special for Tyler and his bride. But what? 'I will think of something' Jack thought, 'and it will be from my heart.'

Ted Boehm and his friend Carlton Wheems, who owned the shop that sold Ted's paintings were opening the wooden crate that held Ted's latest works.

"These landscapes are beautiful," Carlton said as he held up a painting of Sugar Lake. Ted slowly eased out the painting of the Friesian horse. Carlton gasped, hardly able to catch his breath.

"Oh, my lord," he finally whispered. "Ted, this painting is priceless. This must go to the gallery downtown."

"I agree," Ted said, "let's choose five of my best to accompany it, then I must pack my best suit and hurry back to Eau Claire. I have a wedding to attend."

"Whose wedding?" asked Carlton. "A remarkable young deputy sheriff, Tyler Braun and his bride-to-be, Miss Audrey Dixon from Sugar Lake Lodge."

"You made some new friends," Carlton observed.

"They are more like extended family," Ted said smiling.

CHAPTER TWENTY-SEVEN

It was noon, and Ellis was at the bank waiting in line to deposit his paycheck. Looking around he noticed a very nervous young man in the line next to his. The man was sweating and shuffling his feet. One hand was in his jacket pocket, the other held a cloth bag clenched tightly in his fist. Ellis had left his pistol in the patrol car. He didn't like wearing it in the bank, he thought it made other customers nervous. As they neared the teller's window, the nervous man began to pull his hand from his jacket. Without a second thought, Ellis tackled the man!

"What are you doing!" screamed the older woman waiting behind the nervous man. The revolver the man had been reaching for clattered to the floor. Ellis grabbed it and hauled the man to his feet. "Just take it easy, and do what I tell you," Ellis said.

The nervous man just went limp and started crying. "I just need some money to gas up my car," the man sobbed, "my mother is in the hospital in Milwaukee, and I have to get to her!"

Ellis marched the man over to the line of chairs against the wall and sat him down. The bank manager came running over, hands clasped in front of him. "You caught a bank robber," he said. Shaking his head, Ellis said, "No, Mr. Franklin, I stopped a man for questioning, big difference."

"I am so sorry," the nervous man sobbed, "I just needed some money."

"What's your name?" Ellis asked.

"I'm David Hopkins," he said, "am I going to jail now?"

"Let's go see the sheriff," Ellis said, "and you can tell him your story."

Sitting in Sheriff Jeff's office, David told his story. "I live in Fergus Falls, Minnesota," he said. "My father died in 1910 of cancer, so it was just my mother, my sister Joyce and me. I have clerked in the general store for years. Two years ago, Joyce married a young man who worked for the railroad. They moved to Milwaukee, so it was just mother and me. Mother was a librarian, which didn't pay much, but we got by." David stopped, blew his nose, and continued. "Last week my sister called and said she was having their first baby. She wanted mother to be there, and sent a rail ticket. Mother got on the train and Joyce met her at the station. Yesterday Joyce called again and said mother had a stroke, and could I come to Milwaukee." David stopped and dabbed at his leaking eyes. "I just panicked! I ran out of the store, got in my old car and started driving. I ran out of gas this morning here in town with my pockets empty."

"Where did you get the pistol?" Ellis asked.

"It belonged to my father," David said. "Mother doesn't like guns, she didn't want it in the house, so I kept it in my car." There was a long quiet in the sheriff's office, broken only by David's muffled sobs.

"Let me make a phone call," Jeff said.

"He is telling the truth," Jeff told Tyler and Ellis. "I called the hospital in Milwaukee and Mrs. Hopkins is there, along with David's sister Joyce."

"Now what do we do?" Ellis asked.

"He never actually robbed the bank," Tyler said. "In fact, he never got to the teller's window with his gun. A judge would let him go with a warning."

Smiling, Jeff asked, "What are you suggesting Tyler?"

"Just an idea," Tyler said, "If we chip in and buy him a ticket on the next train to Milwaukee, he can pay us back when he returns to pick up his car." Jeff and Ellis looked at each other, then at Tyler.

"I am really going to miss having you and your level head around here." Digging in his pocket, Jeff came out with a five dollar bill. Tyler handed over a ten dollar bill and told Ellis, "Get him something to eat also. I bet he hasn't eaten since Fergus Falls."

THUMP! THUMP! THUMP!

The sound of ears of corn hitting the bang boards as the fall field corn harvest was underway. "I drove the corn wagon for my dad and uncles until I was ten," Nelson Frye told Tyler. The two men stood next to the patrol car watching as a team of horses slowly pulled a wagon through the corn field. An older woman was driving the team, keeping pace with the men as they cut the ears from the stalks and tossed them into the wagon.

"Is that when you started cutting and tossing," asked Tyler.

"Dad gave me my own leather glove with the curved knife on it," Nelson said, "for a farm boy, it was a rite of passage, from boy to young man."

"Does your dad still farm?" Tyler asked.

"No, dad sold the farm three years ago," Nelson said, "after his stroke, dad lost the use of his left arm. His brothers Henry and Albert bought him out, now he and ma just help out where they can. That's ma driving the team."

Roadside stands sprang up around Eau Claire, hay wagons loaded with every kind of produce and fruit grown in the Chippewa valley. Homemade pies and bread were available, and a few sold eggs, churned butter and apple cider. From his pocket, Tyler pulled out a list Julia had given him. He smiled as he checked it over, knowing that she had plenty of vegetables from her own garden. What Julia wanted was apples, pears, berries and jugs of apple cider. Tyler knew that Alma and Audrey were doing the same thing around McKinley, and the pressure cooker in the kitchen at the lodge would be worked overtime. Just thinking of Audrey gave Tyler a warm feeling inside. 'My soon-to-be wife,' he thought, the wedding only days away.

FLU VIRUS DEATHS DECLINING was the headline in the Eau Claire news Leader Telegram. The deadly virus that had spread worldwide and killed millions of people was finally running out of victims. In every country, the death toll was slowly diminishing. The rebuilding of France and Germany was progressing slowly, as families returned to their ruined cities and farms. Every nation that could was sending food, clothing, blankets and medical supplies. Immigrants from Europe chartered ships to bring them to America. Ellis island, in New York harbor was operating around the clock to process the endless lines of people waiting for a better life in the promised land.

"I just got the approval from the city council for another patrol car," Jeff said. He held up the letter. "Deputy Parsons, go see Howard Hale at his car lot and pick out a decent auto for a patrol car." Bradley Parsons took the letter, folded it and put it in his shirt pocket. "Deputy Frye, I want you to man the office today, answer the phone and generally take care of business," Jeff said. "I have four meetings today, starting with the Eau Claire civic improvements Council. Ellis, you and Tyler get out on patrol." Grinning, Ellis said, "Jeff sure has a tough day ahead."

"I hope they buy him lunch," Tyler said, "He gets grumpy if he don't eat."

CHAPTER TWENTY-EIGHT

Jack Porter was waiting at the station when the train arrived. Ted Boehm stepped down, smiling, and said, "Jack, I have a wonderful idea for a wedding gift for Tyler and Audrey."

"So have I," Jack said, "let's get lunch at the cafe and exchange ideas." Over coffee, Jack said, "Let's hear your idea, then I will tell you mine."

"The one thing a young couple need is some privacy," Ted said, "my idea is to build them their own house at Sugar Lake. This would give them a big start at planning for the future." Sipping his coffee, Jack said, "I was thinking along the same line, but a bit different. George and Alma want to be as much a part of their lives as we do. Having them move out of the lodge might take away from that."

Rubbing his chin, Ted said, "that is a point well taken, and I see the logic, but is there another way to help?"

Smiling, Jack said, "I believe there is. If we find a builder to erect two more cabins, Tyler and Audrey will have the entire second floor of the lodge to themselves, without a loss of income." Ted laughed and clapped his hands together.

"Of course!" he exclaimed, "it's the perfect solution! The family would remain intact without any disruption. One cabin a gift from you, the other, a gift from me."

Reaching out his hand, Jack said, "a handshake to seal the deal." Laughing and smiling, the two men shook hands.

Sheriff Jeff Patten returned to his office shaking his head. "Of all the damn fool ideas," he muttered.

"How did the meetings go?" Ellis asked. Dropping his hat onto his desk, Jeff sat. "The City Council and the Civic Improvements people want to expand that strip of land they call an 'airfield' so the city can be ready for an airmail service. There isn't even a building out there!"

"I heard about the airmail taking off between New York and Washington D.C." Tyler said, "but it will cost more than a stamp to use it."

"They want to build an 'airport' building and lengthen the runway and pave it with concrete," Jeff said, "all that costs money, which means all of our taxes go up to pay for it."

"Those Curtiss biplanes can only carry so much weight," Ellis said, "otherwise they can't get off the ground."

"It would also mean flying in all types of weather," Tyler said, "like thunderstorms and snowstorms."

"So far, they are just talking about it," Jeff said, "maybe they will come to their senses and forget the whole thing."

As Tyler and Ellis left, Ellis said, "I bet they didn't buy him lunch, he is grumpy as an old bear."

Jack called George at the lodge and asked him to meet at the cafe in McKinley. "We need your approval for a wedding gift for Tyler and Audrey," he said.

"I don't know what kind of gift would need my approval, but I will certainly meet you," George said. When George arrived, he was greeted by Ted and Jack. When George heard what the plan was, he said, "What a wonderful idea! Alma and I would love to be a part of it, just tell me how we can help."

"First, we need to find a reliable contractor to lay out the site and give us a cost estimate," Jack said.

"Then we need them to start building as soon as possible," Ted added.

"Giles Novak and his sons are the best and most reasonable builders around," George said, "their office is just down the street, let's go talk to them."

Giles Novak was in his office when they got there, "I can come out tomorrow and take a look," he said. "I can have an estimate ready for you in two days." All agreed that was the way to proceed.

Jack explained about the wedding gift, and Giles said, "in that case I will give you my wedding gift discount." Giles said he had been fishing that spring at Sugar Lake. "A pretty young girl with freckles told me where to fish. Is she the one getting married?"

"To a fine young deputy sheriff from Eau Claire," George beamed.

"Then I will have an estimate ready in one day," Giles said with a grin.

True to his word, Giles called and gave Jack an estimate. "That must be some discount," Jack said. "It's less than we had expected. When can you start?"

"My son Leon takes care of the concrete work for the foundations," Giles said, "I'll get him started tomorrow. My other son Vernon does the plumbing and electrical, and I will do the building." Jack found Ted in the garden with Julia. He explained the cost and the timetable. Julia was giggling behind her hands.

"What's so funny" Jack asked.

"If you two grown men could see the looks on your faces right now," she gasped, "you look like two boys who have pulled off the world's best prank." Jack and Ted looked at each other, and all three started laughing.

George told Audrey about the plans for the two new cabins. "It means you and Tyler will have the second floor of the lodge for yourselves," he said, "so you can start redecorating your new home." Audrey broke into tears as she hugged George. "I was worried that Tyler and I would be living out of one room" she said, "what a wonderful gift."

"Jack and Ted came up with the idea," George said, "they insisted on paying for everything. Giles Novak's son Leon will be starting work on the foundations tomorrow."

A timid knock sounded on Jeff's office door. "Yeah, come on in," he said.

David Hopkins stepped into the office, smiling, "Hello sheriff, I am here to pick up my car and pay you back for the train ticket," David said.

"How's your mother doing?" Jeff asked.

"She is recovering nicely" David said, "and I am now an uncle. My sister had her baby, a boy they named Phillip."

Reaching in his desk drawer, Jeff took out David's pistol

and handed it to him. "No thank you sheriff," David said, "I don't want the gun back. It will always remind me of something I would rather forget." From his pocket, David took out two ten dollar bills. "This will pay you back for the train ticket," he said.

Smiling, Jeff said, "I will buy the pistol from you David, how does twenty dollars sound?" smiling, David said, "I accept your offer sheriff, and thank you."

It was late afternoon when Tyler got home. He stood by the porch watching Julia ride in from the field on the gelding.

"I wish I could ride every day," Julia said, stepping down.

"After the wedding, things will settle down," Tyler said, "then you will have more time to ride your horse."

"The gelding is your horse," Julia said.

"Not anymore," Tyler said with a grin, "I am giving him to you. I can't take him with me, and he belongs here with you."

Julia hugged Tyler and kissed his cheek. "Thank you," she said, "I will think of you each time I ride."

As they walked toward the corral, Tyler said, "George, Alma and Audrey will be here tomorrow. Is there anything I can do to help get ready?"

Smiling, Julia said, "everything is ready. I put our other guest, Ted, to work."

"Audrey told me about Jack and Ted having two more cabins built," Tyler said, "I think God must have his hand on my heart to have put me in this place at this time with this family. I am truly blessed."

CHAPTER TWENTY-NINE

The wedding day had arrived. The sun was only a sliver of hazy light on the horizon When Julia and Alma began making breakfast. The two had become fast friends, trading their cooking secrets and sharing precious moments from their pasts. Andy was the first to arrive in the kitchen, with Molly. Tom and Jack soon joined them, followed by Audrey, then Ted, Tyler and George.

"The Friesian mare is restless this morning," Andy said, "she should be ready to foal in a day or two."

"I sure hope it's not today," Jack said, "one special event per day is all I can take." It was a biscuits and gravy breakfast with gallons of coffee.

"Reminds me of the lumber camp," Tyler said with a big grin. Later, Tom and Jack did the dishes while Julia and Alma cleaned up.

Tyler met Mother Superior Veronica at the station. "I am overjoyed to be attending your wedding," she said with a smile, "to see one of my children united with a lovely bride makes my efforts worthwhile."

"For the first time, you will meet all the people who

helped to make this day possible," Tyler told her. As the Packard rolled to a stop in the Porter's yard, Molly was the first to greet her. Then Audrey came forward.

"It means so much to Tyler and I that you are here," she said. Mother met and held hands with George and Alma, Tom and Julia, Jack, Andy and Ted. They all seemed a little awed in her presence, but her easy manner and kind eyes soon put everyone at ease. As they talked, another car drove in. The Reverend Powers arrived, ready for the big event.

At ten minutes until noon, Everyone was gathered in the Porter house parlor. Andy looked uncomfortable but happy in new black dress pants, white shirt and the tie Julia had bought him. Molly sat at his feet with a wide pink ribbon around her neck. Ted was almost formal, in a dark gray suit, silk shirt and bow tie. Julia wore a pale ivory dress with a sash and carried a bouquet of fresh flowers. Alma wore a light blue dress with lace at the neck and shoulders. Mother Superior Veronica looked almost regal in her black habit with brilliant starched white wimple surrounding her face. Jack wore a new suit for the occasion, as did Tom, both black. Tyler had chosen a charcoal gray suit with a black and gray tie against his white shirt. Audrey was beautiful in her simple white dress, her dark hair falling to her shoulders. Against her tan arms and face, the dress seemed to glow. Reverend Powers moved to the front of the room and the ceremony began.

"I now pronounce you man and wife. You may kiss the bride," said Reverend Powers. The tender kiss exchanged between bride and groom signaled the tears and cheers from the gathering. Two orphans who had found each other in an unlikely place at the right time. Mother Veronica watched them, and thanked God for bringing them together. George and Alma hovered over the newlyweds, the joy showing on their shining faces. Jack felt like a proud father, seeing his adopted son being wed. Tom and Julia hugged each other, remembering another time and place. Andy undid his tie and unbuttoned his first two shirt buttons, while Molly let out a short yip, showing her approval. Ted's eyes were misty as he thought of his late wife Alice. 'She would love to have been here,' he thought, remembering his own wedding.

The reception at the Elks Lodge was just getting underway when the Porter's and their guests arrived. A shout went up in the hall, "Make way for the bride and groom!" A shower of rice descended on the laughing couple as they made their way through the crowd. Large white paper bells swung from the ceiling as streamers of all colors raced across from one bell to another. "No champagne or beer, but we have plenty of apple cider and soda" yelled Ellis from the makeshift bar.

A long table was laden with sandwiches, salads, bowls of fresh fruit, dishes of sliced onions, dozens of deviled eggs and baskets of bread and rolls. At least four kinds of cheese had been cut and lay on a plate while cold cuts smothered another plate.

The polka band played, 'Here comes the Bride' as Tyler and Audrey walked to the front of the room.

"Thank you everyone," Tyler shouted, "now dance and have a good time!"

Laying her hand on Jack's arm, Mother Veronica said, "if you would be so kind as to drive me to the station, I must catch the train back to Madison. I will say goodbye to Tyler and Audrey and join you in a moment."

By eight o'clock, the reception was winding down. The guests had eaten and danced and wished the new couple well before leaving. The food table was almost empty and the cider was gone. The band played one last slow waltz as Tyler and Audrey had the floor to themselves.

"I could stay just like this forever," Audrey whispered.

"It still feels like a dream," Tyler said. "Mr. and Mrs. Tyler Braun." The music ended and the band began packing up. "We have a long drive ahead," Tyler said, "but first I need to stop at the house and pack my clothes."

"They are all packed and waiting in the Packard," Audrey said, "Julia and I packed all your things this morning, including your Army uniform."

A basket of cards sat on the table by the door, cards from the guests. Audrey picked it up as the couple left the hall. Sugar Lake Lodge was dark and empty when Tyler and Audrey arrived. "George and Alma are staying one more night with the Porters," Audrey said softly, "I think they wanted us to have the place to ourselves."

"I have never been in your room before," Tyler said shyly.

"The room I had as a single girl is not the room we have now," Audrey said taking Tyler by the hand and walking up the stairs, "Our room has a double bed and a window facing the lake." The bedroom door stood open and the couple entered. Moonlight from a cloudless sky shone on the two young lovers as they embraced.

Tyler woke to the sound of men working. Audrey was already up and dressed, the smell of coffee drifted up from the kitchen. Tyler put on pants and a shirt, walked downstairs and opened the front door. Workmen were removing the forms from the foundations that had been curing. Audrey walked up behind him and held out a cup of steaming coffee.

"Good morning my husband," she said, smiling.

"Good morning my lovely wife," Tyler answered, and kissed her. Two trucks loaded with lumber drove in and parked. Giles Novak stepped down from the lead truck and walked up to the lodge.

"My congratulations to you both," he said smiling, "my crew and I are determined to have your cabins ready before Thanksgiving day, so I will get right to work."

"We thank you Mr. Novak," Tyler said, "anything I can do to help, let me know."

CHAPTER THIRTY

Tyler and Audrey were busy everyday getting the lodge ready for the coming winter. The boats were cleaned and stacked, the grounds raked and the trash burned. Storm windows were put on the lodge to keep heat in and cold out. Wood was cut for the fireplace and the kitchen range, coal was hauled in for the large furnace in the basement. Tyler cleaned out and re-organized the storage shed. Oars, boat cushions and anchors were given their own space. The live bait wells were hosed out and scrubbed. The two new cabins were framed up and the roof of each was shingled. They would be ready before the snow came.

Audrey was a cyclone of cleaning. "Jack, Julia and Tom are coming to stay overnight, and this lodge will sparkle."

Alma was baking, humming as she worked. Having Tyler at the lodge eased her mind about George overworking. The young man seemed to have the energy of three people. Alma was delighted to have guests, especially the Porters. What wonderful people! She smiled to herself thinking of Audrey and how happy she was with Tyler. In the evenings George and Alma would sit in the parlor with the couple as Tyler told stories of his days in the lumber camp. It was a magical time for all.

The Porters were given a tour of Sugar Lake Lodge and the cabins. "They're almost done," Jack said, "Giles has kept his word."

"They worked from sun up to sun down," Tyler told him, "and Giles put a ceiling-mounted curtain divider in each one, so two couples can share, if necessary."

"I want to update the kitchen at the Porter house," Jack said. "I'll have to give Giles a call."

Tom had a fire going in the fireplace when they returned to the lodge. "Julia and I want to spend a few days here next summer," Tom said, "it's so peaceful and relaxing."

"If you can get Andy away from the forge, bring him along," Audrey said, "and don't forget Molly."

"I have some wonderful news from Ted," Julia said, his painting of the Friesian mare was exhibited at the gallery in Milwaukee, and he titled it 'Porter Farms Friesian.' He has been offered $50,000 for it!" Everyone was stunned!

Jack said, "The Friesian mare foaled another female, and I have been getting offers from as far away as California for her foals. Porter Farms is becoming known nationwide as a place to get quality horses."

"We have eight bottles of fine Oshkosh beer," Audrey said, "Let's toast Ted and Porter Farms!"

The cabins were finished. Giles gave a tour of them, pointing out some finer points. "I put in double pane windows to keep them warmer, and added some extra insulation on the north walls" he said proudly. Both cabins were a bit larger than the others, offering more sleeping space. "Audrey and I were talking," Tyler said, "and the other three cabins could use an updating. Could you do that in the spring?"

"The middle of April would be a good time to do that," Giles said, "I will look them over and give you an estimate."

It was the weekend before Thanksgiving when Audrey and Alma returned from McKinley with the news.

"The doctor says I am definitely pregnant," Audrey said blushing slightly, "he expects early July as a due date." Tyler hugged her with tears misting his eyes.

"We are going to have a grandchild," Alma told George.

"We must call the Porters and tell them," Audrey said.

"And I will call Mother Superior Veronica," Tyler said.

George held up a slip of paper saying "Ted Boehm called while everyone was out. He is coming for a visit on Thanksgiving."

Laughing, Tyler said, "Ted's timing is perfect. We will give him the news then."

Ted was overjoyed. "The child will lack for nothing," he said. "He will be like my own grandchild."

"How are your paintings doing at the gallery?" Tyler asked.

"My paintings are doing so well, I had to hire an accountant to keep up," Ted said laughing, "Now, I still want to do a painting of the Brauns. You two are the perfect couple to sit for a portrait."

"How long will it take?" Tyler asked.

"I only need you to sit for the sketch," Ted said, "the painting will come later."

"That has got to be the biggest chicken I have ever seen," Tyler said. He was watching Alma and Audrey preparing Thanksgiving dinner.

"Frank Tilly and his wife Doris raise Wyandotte chickens," Alma told him. "The hens weigh about eight pounds and the roosters get as large as ten pounds, which this one is."

"The meat is so tender and tasty, there are seldom leftovers," Audrey told him. As the table was laid for the dinner, Ted marveled at the food. Cranberry sauce, stuffing, sweet potatoes, white potatoes, gravy, dinner rolls, green beans and an apple & walnut salad. For dessert, three kinds of pie. Apple, pumpkin and mincemeat. Everyone gathered around the dining room table and sat. They joined hands and bowed their heads as George said grace.

Julia was sewing diapers. The Singer treadle machine was getting a workout as the white squares were doubled and hemmed. A box lay open on a chair next to her. I was already half full of knitted booties and little caps. She hummed as she pushed the cloth through the machine, happy to be sewing for a child. 'It will be our grandchild,' she thought, 'regardless of birth.' Jack was reading the newspaper, and Tom was going over the accounts. Glancing over at the clock, Julia realized it was time to begin supper.

For this cold November day, chicken and dumplings would grace the table, the last of the chicken left from Thanksgiving dinner. Tyler and Audrey had a call, letting her know that Ted was there to begin a painting.

Turning to Tom she said, "We must visit the lodge before Christmas. I will let you know when my gift box is full."

Looking up from the paper, Jack said, "that reminds me, I have some shopping to do."

Laughing, Julia said, "A fishing rod and reel are not an appropriate gift for a baby not yet born,"

"Darn it" Jack sighed, "now I have to think of another gift."

Looking out the window into the darkness, Tyler watched the first snowfall of December drift lazily to the ground. Audrey and Alma were making a list of the baby's needs. Ted and George were playing chess, and both were sipping hot apple cider. Tyler thought back on his life, remembering his days at the orphanage with Mary and Mother Superior Veronica. He and Audrey had already decided on a name for the baby. If it was a girl, she would be named Mary, if a boy was born, he would be named Louis.

His thoughts drifted on to the war, and the battles he had fought. The strong memory of meeting the Porter's, and how they had accepted him into their family. Then, his mind bought the lumber camp into focus, and the days of cutting and hauling logs for the mill in Wausau. His days as a deputy sheriff followed, both good times and not so good times. The sharpest memory was meeting Audrey, their first time on the lake when they both realized their paths in life would become the same path. Now, a child would soon be born to them.

'Thank you God,' Tyler thought, 'for all that you have given me. My life is full, and it has only just begun.'

The End

ABOUT THE AUTHOR

Mark Gengler was born and raised on a small farm north of Medford, Wisconsin. He joined the U.S. Army in 1963 and was stationed at Fort Bragg, N.C., with the 82nd Airborne Division. He saw action in the Dominican Republic in 1965. After his discharge, he traveled America, working odd jobs in California, Texas, Colorado, Kansas City and New Orleans. He returned to Wisconsin and went to broadcasting school on the G.I. Bill. Mr. Gengler was a disc-jockey, got married, and went to work at the University of Wisconsin, Oshkosh, until retiring in 2003.